THREE HEARTS HIDEAWAY

Paperback ISBN: 978-1-7381324-0-9

E-book ISBN: 978-1-7381324-1-6

Edited by: Jacqui Nelson

Proofread by: Caroline Palmier, Love & Edits

Cover art by: Brittany Keller, @brittanykellerart

First paperback edition February 2024.

Website: www.lunadayauthor.com

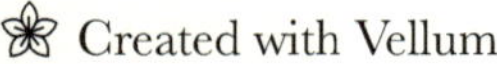

THREE HEARTS HIDEAWAY

LUNA DAY

Content Warnings

This story features explicit sexual content and strong language. It is intended for an audience 18+. There is on-page narcissistic/verbally abusive behaviour, kink-shaming, slut-shaming, one scene of consensual non-consent (with explicit consent and a safe word), sex without a condom (consensual), and one scene of minor physical violence.

To anyone who ever felt like sex was something to be ashamed of. This is for you.

Chapter One

AVA

She didn't expect Little Greenfield to be so…little.

This was why she usually made detailed travel plans: so she didn't end up in an unfamiliar town with a single carry-on suitcase and a lot of regret.

Sitting on the only shuttle from the rinky-dink airport, Ava Anderson was thankful she'd arrived on a Tuesday—one of the few days the airport ran a shuttle into town. A happy coincidence in her otherwise disaster of a day.

She took stock of her surroundings while chastising herself for being so rash. Little Greenfield had one five-block long road with shops and amenities, while the rest appeared residential. Surely, it would have a hotel she could check into. Another reason she normally made travel plans: so she definitely had a place to stay when she arrived at her destination.

Yesterday, when her phone's entire contact list received a voice message from her dickbag boyfriend—now *ex*-boyfriend—spilling all her sexual fantasies and sordid secrets, she decided to make herself scarce. Initially, she scrolled through her contacts for someone to talk to. Someone who could help her get through the embarrassment she was dealing with. But there was no one.

She'd pushed away her two best friends long ago. So she couldn't call Brittany. Not Layla, either. Not after giving them the silent treatment for the better part of a year. How Sebastian had managed to get her to stop speaking to the two most important friends in her life, she didn't know. He manipulated her so expertly that she didn't realize it until the damage was done. She saw that now.

It wasn't like her to head somewhere unknown at the drop of a hat. But a mini-sabbatical away from Sebastian, away from her job, and away from Ottawa seemed like a good idea. She couldn't believe she'd left the next day without booking any accommodations or checking to see if there was a hotel. For all that was holy, she was a senior project manager at the second largest marketing firm in the capital of the country. She knew her shit! Her work life was immaculate. But her personal life? At this point in time, it was a disaster. No close friends. No boyfriend. Taking off without proper planning. She shook her head, disconcerted with how she'd landed in this position.

She'd never been to Little Greenfield, but it sounded cozy and off the beaten path. A good place to get away and puzzle out exactly what she wanted in a partner. Because of the prick Sebastian, who was decidedly not a good partner, everyone she knew was laughing at her.

Or was disgusted with her.

Or was too embarrassed to look her in the eye.

Her mom and dad got that voice message. They'd called, of course, to let her know they'd stopped listening at the first mention of the word *slut*. They also not-so-subtly suggested she leave Sebastian. She thanked the universe that they lived in Toronto. That conversation face-to-face would've been way more awkward.

Not to mention her colleagues, clients, her building manager, and her boss. They all got the voice message, too.

Using her banked paid personal days to take time off work was easier than imagined. Her boss could hardly meet her eyes when he hastily approved her request for ten days off.

She would kill Sebastian. Or cut off his balls. Or egg his house.

But she wouldn't do anything, because she never did. Standing up to Sebastian was like a Tonka truck standing up to a bulldozer. She'd never hold up. She wouldn't even make a dent. What he did was unforgivable. She had no way to undo it, so she'd finally mustered enough courage to dump his not-sorry ass and fled the city. Thank goodness she'd had the sense to say *no* when he'd tried to convince her to move in with him six months ago. He'd been making her feel stupid about her choice ever since, but boy was it saving her ass now.

The shuttle stopped outside a post office. The four other passengers piled off, and the driver announced this was the only stop the service made.

"Any chance there's a hotel around here?" she asked the driver.

"Of course, darlin'. Best hotel in town is two blocks that way." He gestured straight in front of him. "It's also the only hotel." He gave a wry chuckle, clearly pleased with himself.

"I appreciate that, thank you," she said, exiting the bus.

"Not sure there will be anything available this time of year, though."

His comment stopped her in her tracks. Nothing available? At all? "Sorry, what time of year is it? Why wouldn't I be able to get a room?"

"On account of the fishing competition. Best fishing in the area is right here in Little Greenfield at Kawawaymog Lake. Heck, I'd say it's the best fishing in Ontario, but I'm biased." He winked.

"How long does the competition last?"

"Oh, it starts tomorrow and goes for a week. The other passengers are here for that reason. Now is the prime time for our fishing tourists."

Great. She was having a poorly planned, quarter-life crisis in a remote town, and it had a boatload of fishermen booked into the one hotel. Once again, she scolded herself for being so thoughtless.

"Thanks for the heads up. I guess I'll have to take my chances." Dejected, she set off toward the only hotel in town, suitcase in hand.

The Quiet Shore Hotel had a worn white façade, green wooden shutters lining each window, and a happy little plant sitting next to the entrance. Noticeably well taken care of. That buoyed her spirits, and she hoped the people inside were good caretakers, too. Maybe they could squeeze her in somewhere.

She entered the bright lobby to the scent of fresh coffee. A cozy sitting area by a fireplace sat across from the reception desk, where an older lady spoke to the passengers from the shuttle. Her heart dropped. The driver was probably right about the hotel being full, too.

When the customers made their way up the stairs to the left of the desk, she stepped forward and did her best to flash a prize-winning smile.

"How can I help you, dear?" the lady whose name tag read *Gertie* asked with a warm smile. Her short salt-and-pepper curls and bright emerald earrings stood out against her umber skin.

She wrung her hands. "I don't have a reservation, but maybe you have something available? I'm hoping to stay for at least a week. Ten days at most."

"Oh shucks." Gertie's brows furrowed. "My hotel is full, I'm afraid."

Just her luck. One hotel in town and no rooms. Damn fishing competition. There had to be something available.

Anxiety crept up her neck, causing the muscles at the base of her skull to tighten. "I'll take anything." She couldn't stop wringing her hands. "Even a back room or storage space. I didn't plan ahead, and I always plan ahead. I read *Little Greenfield* on the flight board and it sounded so comfortable, and—"

Gertie placed her hand on Ava's shoulder, stopping her tirade. Her eyes focused softly on her own. "I wish I could help you out, hun, but there really aren't any rooms available."

Discouraged, tears stung her eyes. "I'm not in an ideal situation right now and would really love to catch a break." She glanced down and began to mumble her thanks before turning to go.

"Oh, please don't cry." Gertie left her spot behind the desk and put her arm around her. "I don't know what's going on in your life, but I know that when we have the chance to do good for others, we take it. That's something Harold, my late husband, used to say. We ran this hotel together for forty years." That warm smile illuminated her face once more. "I'll see what I can do. In the meantime, you're welcome to relax in the lobby. Or there is a friendly pub across the road where you can get a bite to eat. You can leave your suitcase with me behind the counter, if you'd like."

Gertie quickly became her favourite person. Genial, lovely, caring. Just what she needed at this juncture in her life.

"Thanks, Gertie. That sounds like a good plan. I do need something to eat." She tucked her suitcase behind the reception desk, and with a promise from Gertie to grab her from the pub if the woman figured something out, she made her way across the street to The White Pine Pub.

Little Greenfield only had one of everything, it seemed. One hotel. One pub. Probably one grocery store, one restaurant, one library—if any. It would be charming if she didn't think she'd be sleeping on the streets tonight.

Like the hotel, the pub was old, but the outside appeared recently painted. The inside boasted a classic, yet comfortable feel. Lovely and dark, with light spilling out from lamps behind the bar off to the left, and exposed bulb fixtures above the tables. Heavy drapes covered the windows, but they didn't make it stuffy. It had the air of being snug and…sultry. Could you describe a place as sultry? Why not? Such a masculine space, but done in such a tasteful way any person would enjoy being here.

The exposed dark wood beams matched the wood of the bar counter. Black wooden swivel chairs lined the polished bar. Round tables with metal stools dotted the floor. A few booths were tucked into the far wall. Tiny, ornate birdcages sat atop each table with a tea light inside. An interesting detail that added to the appeal of the place.

Considering it was only three in the afternoon, the place was pretty empty. She counted the total number of people on one hand.

Plopping herself down at the bar, she scanned the room once more to find a server. No one stood out. Small sleepy town, slow sleepy service.

Maybe she'd put her head down on the bartop, take a quick nap, and Gertie would wake her when her accommodation problem was solved. That seemed reasonable, if not a little unhinged. Who hasn't slept in a pub in a town they've never been to that they bought a one-way ticket to earlier that morning? Probably no one, that's who.

Resting her head on the bar, she tucked her purse tightly between her legs to keep it safe and closed her eyes. The last two days had been an absolute shit show, and a bit of mediocre rest to calm her mind and figure out what the hell she needed to do about everything sounded fantastic.

"Welcome to my pub. Can I get you something?" A deep voice rumbled from behind the bar, a hint of amusement in the velvety tone.

Her eyes went wide. She slowly unglued her forehead from the bartop and looked up to see who the attractive voice belonged to. How she kept her jaw from dropping, she didn't know.

His hair hung down to his shoulders, brunette with a slight wave, and he had a light bronze complexion. A thick, well-groomed beard hugged his face. Black tattoos wrapped around his neck and disappeared beneath his faded t-shirt, reappearing on his biceps, and snaking down the entirety of his arms. Even the back of his hands had intricate designs. A medley of flowers. Unexpected, but she liked it.

He was in the ballpark of six feet tall, broad, and built like a truck. Tall, thick, and tattooed. Her holy trifecta.

What the hell was her dream man doing in a place she'd never once dreamed about? Was this her mind's way of making her feel better after the horrendous last few days? It wouldn't be out of the ordinary for her brain to short circuit to get her through a tough time. But no…this man was real and standing in front of her, patiently waiting for her to respond.

"Um…sorry, what did you say?" No point in trying to hide that she spent the last thirty seconds ogling him instead of focusing on his question.

A grin tugged at his lips and he asked again, "Is there something I can get you?"

"Right. A gin and tonic would be good."

"Coming right up," he said with a wink, turning to fetch the fixings from the shelves and mix the drink.

Holy Lord Almighty.

Seriously.

Who else could have crafted the specimen in front of her?

Sleeping on the street in Little Greenfield wasn't looking quite so bad after all. If it meant seeing this beefcake every day, she would get on board with sleeping on the cold, hard ground.

She had about five seconds to compose herself before he would be in front of her with her drink.

"So what brings you to town?" he asked, setting her drink in front of her.

"Oh, just here for a visit. You know, fishing competition and all that," she answered hastily, absently gesturing about the room.

He looked at her—really looked at her—taking everything in with his deep-brown eyes. A second passed before he burst out laughing.

"I'm so sorry, but there is no way in hell you're here for the fishing competition."

Ava let out a deep sigh and her chest felt a fraction

lighter. She guessed she'd been holding it in for a while. "That obvious, eh?"

He nodded.

"It's a long story."

The hot bartender shrugged. "I've got time."

She raised her eyebrow. "I don't even know your name and you want to hear about my problems?"

"It's Roman Banks, and yes, I want to hear about your problems. Because if a gorgeous girl like you is in Little Greenfield, there's gotta be a good reason. Not that I'm complaining."

"Ava Anderson." She reached out and shook Roman's hand across the bar. A rush of warmth coursed through her arm at the contact, and she swore her heart skipped a beat. "Buckle up, Roman. This ride is a wild one."

Chapter Two

AVA

She reccunted the last two days to Roman as briefly as possible. No need to go into all the nitty-gritty details. The gist would do it.

She told him how she finally talked to Sebastian about what she felt was missing in their…intimate times together, omitting the specifics, of course. And how he immediately reacted like she'd slapped his face. Shock, followed by disbelief, then anger. Sebastian had made her feel dirty and ashamed, like something was wrong with her. He berated her until she was in tears on the floor, slamming the door on his way out.

Sebastian sent his voice message that same evening. After the disbelief wore off, she gathered the strength to dump him the next day and immediately hopped on a flight to the first place that sounded inviting—Little Greenfield.

"Let me get this straight. He sent a voice message to everyone on your contact list? Not a text, but a recording?" Roman was fully engrossed in her story. During her tale, he'd made his way around the bar and was now sitting on the stool next to her.

She nodded. "For some reason, that made it a lot more personal. It hurt me more that way. I think he knew it would."

"And he sent it to you, too?"

Again, she nodded.

"What a fucking coward," he fumed, shaking his head.

Not the reaction she was expecting. "I'd say he's a jerk. A jackass. A prick. All those things. But a coward? It takes balls to send a message like that to almost one hundred people."

"First, Ava,"—Roman placed his hand on her knee and swiveled her chair so she faced him, sending her heart backflipping into her stomach—"he's a coward because he sent a fucking voice message to everyone you know. He hid behind technology instead of talking to you face-to-face. Second, he's a coward because he obviously feels threatened by you. He didn't try to understand where you're coming from. He took what you shared and used it against you because he's not a man. He's a little boy who can't understand a partner having needs that differ from his own."

She stared at him, speechless. Not only was he drop dead gorgeous, but he had a heart of gold too? Perhaps she should thank Sebastian. Well…she wouldn't go that far. Sebastian was still an absolute ass. How it took her this long to realize that was disappointing. But without his idiocy, and a much-needed wakeup call, she wouldn't be in front of this absolutely perfect specimen of a man right now.

"Thank you. I…I needed to hear that."

"Anytime. It's the truth." He swiveled her to face the bar again, got up, and checked on the other few tables before returning to make her another drink.

"So, you ran away. Now what?" he asked, his eyes searching hers.

She let out a demoralized laugh and took a sip of her second gin and tonic. "Now I need a place to stay while I sort out my personal life. I didn't think any of this through." She grimaced. "Gertie is trying to work something out for me, but considering she hasn't popped by yet, I'm not holding my breath."

Roman smiled what seemed like a genuine, caring smile, and fished his phone out of his pocket. "One second." He held up his finger and disappeared into the back room.

Downing the last of her drink, she let herself

wallow in her predicament a moment longer. Maybe she'd take her parents up on their offer to stay with them. Not that she didn't love her mom and dad to pieces, but staying with them for a prolonged period of time was not something she wanted to do as a thirty-three-year-old woman. Neither was explaining the sexual content of Sebastian's voice message in-person. But if it was a better option, then—

"Oh darling, I came as soon as I could!" Gertie called as she entered the pub, interrupting her thoughts. Her chandelier earrings swaying with each step, she made a beeline for Ava.

"Bad news or good news?" Ava asked, fearing she already knew which it would be.

Gertie pursed her lips. "Mostly bad, I'm afraid. I can't finagle a room for you at the hotel this week. The good news is, after the fishing competition is over, we're wide open. You can have your pick of rooms."

"I appreciate your help. I'm sure I'll figure something out."

"I can call a few ladies from my mahjong group, but I wanted to check if you're comfortable with that first. I'm sure one of them has a spare bedroom or couch to sleep on for a few days. Or we could check hotels in Huntsville? It's a town about an hour south of—"

"That won't be necessary, Gertie," Roman's deep voice rumbled from the back room. As he emerged, a brilliant smile filled his face. "We can put her up."

Gertie clicked her tongue. "Oh, why didn't I think of that? Logan's done renovating the guest suites, then?"

"Not quite, but that shouldn't matter. Ava can use the facilities in the back house if she needs."

"And you don't think Logan will mind?"

"Just got off the phone with him. It took a bit of convincing, but he says he's fine with it."

Who was Logan? What guest suites? It's like they had forgotten she was sitting right there.

"Hi." Ava waved her hand. "Can someone please clue me in here?"

Gertie beamed at her. "I can't think of a better place for you to stay, and with two of the nicest fellas I've ever met."

Ava shot Roman a quick glance, seeking clarification.

"Logan King is my best friend, roommate, and business partner. We have an extra space you can stay in for as long as you need. That's why I stepped away. I wanted to confirm it would work before I got your hopes up, but you're in luck. You can stay with us."

Her eyes felt like they were bugging out of her head. Her mouth hung open in astonishment.

Roman must have confused her complete shock for worry because he quickly added, "If you want to, that is. Or you could stay with a friend of Gertie's instead. If they are available and you prefer. No pressure. I get that we're two random men and—"

"No, no! Not that I don't appreciate Gertie's offer." She turned to the sweet woman standing at her side. "You've been so kind to me. But I wouldn't want to put out one of your friends if I don't have to. It sounds like Roman has room to accommodate me, and I don't want to be a burden. Is that alright?"

"Of course, dear." She patted her hand. "I trust these fellas completely. They've helped me out of more than a couple of jams. I'll be at the hotel if you need anything else. Don't hesitate to stop by!" Gertie spun on her heel and made her way across the street to her hotel.

Ava would take her up on her offer to stop by. She'd bring her a small gift to say thank-you.

"So…you're good to stay with us, then?" Roman asked from behind the bar.

"I already like you and so does Gertie, so I'll take my chances. How much do you want?" she asked, opening the banking application on her phone. "I can send you a money transfer right now, so you don't have to worry about me paying when I leave."

"Don't worry about it, Ava."

Her eyebrows drew together. "I insist. I can't put you out and not compensate you. You're already doing me a huge favour."

"Well, if you insist, let me talk to Logan and we'll work something out together."

She felt better about that. No way she could stay

with these guys and not pay them for their accommodations. "So, will I like this Logan guy?" she teased.

Roman laughed and made a strangled noise that lodged in his throat. Like he was trying to suppress the sound coming out of his beautiful mouth. She wasn't sure what to make of it, but it didn't seem reassuring.

"Well, you like me," he said, flashing his dazzling smile once again. "And Logan is 100% the opposite of me."

"Honestly, as long as I have a bed, a shower, and a toilet, I'm satisfied. Thank you, again."

"Don't thank me yet. I can only give you one out of three of those things," he happily stated and ducked into the back room once more.

"Wait, one? What do you mean? You have a toilet, right?" she called after him.

They drove in Roman's vintage Chevy Cheyenne to the outskirts of town, which took less than ten minutes. Turning down a dirt road surrounded by forest, they emerged into a clearing where rich brown timber beams rose to form a breathtaking two-story cabin. She wasn't even sure it could be called that. It stood so much bigger than what she would typically picture a cabin to be.

When Roman told her on the drive that he and

Logan owned a bed and breakfast they were opening in a few months, this wasn't what she expected.

A large deck appeared to wrap around each side. Brushed bronze sconces lined the outside walls, creating a welcoming glow. Floor-to-ceiling windows flanking the front doors further contributed to the impressive building.

Deep-green pines stretched on all sides as far as she could see. The ground was littered with dried needles, creating a blanket of brown and orange. The late September air smelled fresh and earthy. The perfect autumn backdrop for the beautiful building in front of her.

Ava exited the truck. She stood staring at the giant log cabin in front of her, taking it in. It might've been one of the most magnificent buildings she'd ever seen. She rounded the back of the pickup to retrieve her single piece of luggage. "Your place is gorgeous."

Roman put out a hand to stop her, and grabbed her suitcase from the truck bed. "Thanks. It's taken a lot of work."

She allowed him to help her, appreciating the kind gesture. "Work? You mean you built this?" Her face must have given away how dumbstruck she was, because Roman let out a laugh.

"Well, Logan and I did. I can't take *all* the credit." He headed toward the front door.

"It's magnificent. I can't believe you made this," she said, quickly drawing alongside him.

"It's the fourth bed and breakfast we've built. There are two others in Ontario and one in Quebec, so we figured we'd build one for ourselves. Give it a go. See if we can make some supplemental income between projects."

She noticed two other trucks parked in the lot. "Are other people staying here, too?"

He shook his head. "You're our first guest. Why do you ask?"

She pointed at the other vehicles parked beside Roman's.

"Those are just our work trucks. We use them for the construction business."

They entered through the front doors together, and her jaw dropped for the second time that day.

Behind the welcome desk was a living room with overstuffed couches and plush armchairs. A grandiose stone fireplace occupied a good portion of the wall, extending to the top of what she guessed were sixteen foot ceilings. An area rug of greens, browns, and creams anchored the space and added to its coziness.

"What's it called?"

"What?"

"Your bed and breakfast. Does it have a name?"

"Not yet. That's one thing Logan and I can't seem to agree on."

At the back of the house was a full kitchen with well-oiled butcher block countertops and white oak cabinets. Five leather stools were neatly tucked beneath a breakfast bar. Next to it was a dining area with four small, round tables and matching chairs.

A grand staircase sat in the middle of everything, with intricately carved wood railings and an elegant runner drawing the eye toward the second floor, which was open to the rest of the house. She counted three large doors—one on the left, one in the middle, and one on the right—that most likely led to bedrooms, and several smaller doors that she guessed were closets, storage, or bathrooms.

"You're letting me stay here?" No way there wasn't a catch. Sure, she was paying, but this place was way too nice.

Roman shrugged. "You need a place to stay, and we have the room. The guest suites aren't completely finished, though. So you're going to have to deal with a few inconveniences."

She nodded, eager to show that a bother here or there was nothing to her. He was hot and generous. This impromptu getaway was seeming better by the minute. "A few inconveniences aren't a problem."

"Good. Because none of the guest rooms have the plumbing fully installed yet."

She stared at him. No plumbing. Wait…no toilet?

"So I'm supposed to go…" She didn't know how to finish that sentence.

A deep chuckle rumbled from his throat. "Don't worry. You don't have to go in the trees or anything.

But you'll have to use the bathroom Logan and I share."

An alleviated sigh left her lips. "Thank goodness. That's fine with me."

Was it absurd to say sharing a bathroom with Roman made her a bit excited? He was definitely hot, easily checking all her boxes. What would he look like coming out of a steamy washroom in nothing but a towel? Her cheeks started to flush.

"So you can choose to stay in any of the upstairs guest rooms. They're more or less the same. We haven't quite gotten to painting or decorating them yet. But you'll have a bed and a dresser, as well as a personal balcony with a magnificent view of the forest."

He set her luggage on the staircase. "I'll bring that upstairs for you in a minute," he said, gesturing for her to follow him to the kitchen, where he pressed a panel and it opened ever-so-slightly.

Roman wiggled his eyebrows as he pulled open the panel to reveal a disguised doorway and waited to see her reaction.

"A hidden door!" She couldn't contain her excitement. Who hasn't wished for their home to have a hidden passageway that leads to a secret library or a moody speakeasy? "Where does it go?" she asked eagerly.

His expression lit up, clearly proud of this place,

and she didn't blame him. She'd only seen the main area, and she was more than impressed.

"I'll show you." Roman offered his hand.

She took it, and his grip tightened around hers. The contact sent sparks through her fingers, and a cascade of butterflies took flight within her stomach. With one simple touch igniting her insides, it was hard not to wonder what a whole lot more could do.

Chapter Three

ROMAN

Roman flipped on the lights and led Ava into the back house. The hallway stretched on either side of them, with a door leading to his room at one end, Logan's at the other, and a large shared bathroom in the middle.

He was over the moon about how well Logan and he had concealed what they called their *owners' suites*.

The hidden door was his idea.

It allowed them to have a separate living space, away from any guests, and afforded them their own privacy. Maintaining a small boundary between their working life and their personal space was important.

"You can use our bathroom here," he said, opening the door to show Ava.

She gaped at the sight in front of her. Even with

her mouth wide open, she was absolutely beautiful. A summer tan kissed her ivory skin, freckles dotted her nose and cheeks, and her blue eyes sparkled in a way he'd never seen before, like they were dancing in the light.

He thought Logan went overboard when designing their washroom, but seeing Ava's expression was worth it. Leave it to Logan not to listen to reason when it came to his own luxury. That man was a sucker for the finer things.

Charcoal-coloured stone tile covered the floor and the walls. The shower, separated by floor to ceiling glass, filled the entire rear of the room. Multiple rainfall shower heads were placed strategically inside, along with a stone bench.

On the left and right, they each had their own dark granite counter with raised stone sinks opposite each other. He was embarrassed at the sight of his unorganized, and frankly messy, toiletries littered across the counter. A stark contrast to Logan's minimalist belongings arranged in a neat row according to size. At least his towels were inside the towel warmer and not thrown on top, like usual.

He tried to imagine seeing it from Ava's perspective. Yeah…overboard for two bachelors. Probably not what she expected to see.

"I'll tidy my side and you can put your stuff in here. Best to leave Logan's side alone. He'll blow a gasket if anything gets out of order." He made it sound like a joke, but Logan would truly freak out.

She nodded, roaming the space, examining the luxury of it all. "Thank you. I don't…wow. I didn't expect a bathroom that looked like a spa."

"Well, that's all Logan. He designs the spaces, then we build them together. I'd be happy with four walls, a shower, and a toilet, but that's not how he operates."

Guiding Ava out of the washroom, he directed her gaze down the hallway. "My room is down there. If you need anything, ask. Logan is at the opposite end of the hall. Best not to go in there. He's pretty particular."

"Particular?" she asked, raising one eyebrow and quirking her lips.

God, that was cute.

"You'll see what I mean soon enough. Come on, let's get you settled in one of the guest rooms."

He led Ava through the secret doorway and up to where she'd be staying, snatching her suitcase for her along the way. His mother had always taught him to be a proper gentleman. If someone needed help, you helped. Whether that be as big as letting a stranger stay at your home, or as small as carrying a piece of luggage. A person got back what they put into the world, plain and simple.

Ava chose the door at the top of the stairs and he encouraged her to enter. What he really wanted to do was show her his room, though. Not because it was impressive in any sort of way, but because his brain kept picturing her knocking on his door late at night, wearing nothing but a t-shirt and thong, and asking for his help with something more…personal. And while having her actually stand in his room would be nothing like that fantasy, it would be one step closer.

But he didn't want to come off like a pervy loser. Ava deserved better than that. Especially since the last man in her life was already a Grade A asshole, and she was here to get away. At least, that's what she'd told him.

He smiled at her. "I'll leave you to it, then. Make yourself comfortable. Logan is on his way with pizza. I'll grab you when he arrives."

"Thanks. You have no idea how much I appreciate this. And you don't have to escort me to supper. Holler up to me, and I'll join you."

Roman made his way downstairs to give her some privacy. He'd known this woman all of one day, and he was already feeling smitten. There was something about her. Was it the lilting sound of her voice? The bounce in her blonde curls? Or the way her bright eyes peered at him when he offered her a place to stay—as if he was everything to her at that moment? Or maybe it was how she'd spoken openly to him at the pub, putting her trust in a stranger? She'd let herself be vulnerable. He didn't normally sit and talk with bar patrons while he was working. But Ava was easy to talk to, and he felt like she needed a listening ear.

He had to slow his roll.

In the kitchen, he grabbed a beer from the fridge and cracked it open. Had he been alone for a long time? Yes. Was he tired of being single at thirty-five? Of course. And was he ready to settle down?

Absolutely.

He was tired of feeling stagnant. Not a lot of fresh blood passed through Little Greenfield, and he hadn't had any sort of proper relationship in a long while.

Maybe this could be something? He ran his palm over his beard. He swore she was making eyes at him in the bar. He wanted her to want him. That didn't mean she actually wanted him. Making those kinds of assumptions wasn't helpful for anybody.

But, God, he needed forward projection in his life. He didn't want to live with Logan forever in their rustic B&B like a pair of permanent bachelors. Perhaps this was the start of that momentum? He could show Ava that not all guys were closed-minded pricks.

The front door opened and Roman turned his attention to Logan carrying two large pizzas into the house.

Okay. Specifically, that *he* wasn't a prick. He couldn't say the same for Logan, though he had his reasons for being so guarded.

Logan wouldn't help make his case for men in

general. His disposition was downright sour at the best of times. And Roman was sure this wouldn't be an exception.

AVA

Ava threw her carry-on suitcase on the bed and plopped down next to it. Paint cans and tarps were in one corner, a mirror laying on the floor beside the dresser in another corner. A big, cushy snuggle chair sat overlooking the glass doors that led to the balcony. That was an appreciated touch. She'd definitely be spending time there, nestled in a nice fuzzy blanket.

The view out the floor to ceiling glass doors was breathtaking. All the way to the horizon consisted mostly of eastern white pine trees, but the occasional larch dotted the landscape, the leaves already turning yellow. The sun was just beginning to set. Days were getting shorter now that fall was here. The fading light gave the earth a stunning golden glow.

There wasn't any furniture on the balcony. Maybe Roman would let her help pick something out? He did say they hadn't decided on decor for the rooms yet. Maybe she could help while she was here. Earn her keep by doing more than paying for the room. She'd be happy to assemble some tables and chairs, put together a backsplash, or hang a picture or two.

Turning to survey the room, she noticed a stack of tile sitting inside the bathroom doorway. Upon inspection, it was a sleek, modern white marble. After seeing the guys' washroom, this kind of poshness didn't surprise her. But Roman didn't strike her as someone whose first pick for a backsplash was Carrara marble. She'd like to think he'd choose an earthy coloured stone. Textured, but still classy.

He was probably a get-your-hands-dirty type of guy, but in a good way. Like he didn't mind hard work and was always the first one to volunteer to help, no matter what the situation was. Like how he jumped at the chance to come to her aid.

She flopped down on the bed and stared at the ceiling. Look at her. She rolled into town completely unprepared, didn't know a soul, and Roman rescued her after an hour of conversation. He was living proof there were good men in this world. And after being repeatedly gaslighted by Sebastian for two years, that was something she needed to believe in right now.

It didn't hurt that he was sexy as sin and built like a tank. On more than one occasion today, she'd caught herself thinking about how easily he could lift her and throw her on his bed. How his powerful hands could effortlessly restrain her. How he could surely make her choke on his big co—

Okay, it's possible Sebastian was right. Maybe her desires were a bit…different.

But did that matter? A loving partner would be

open to trying out her kinks before writing them off. Or at least hearing what they were and why she liked them. Instead, Sebastian had tried to make her feel dirty. Ashamed.

When she finally got the guts to reveal her fantasies, he told her she wasn't normal. The word *deviant* was used several times. He actually yelled that she was broken, that she must have a screw loose, because *people shouldn't want the things she wanted.* It took two years together for her to open up. A little part of her must've known he'd react that way.

This time away needed to be productive. Ten days to figure out who she was and what she really wanted in a partner without Sebastian's voice in her ear, constantly trying to control her.

The bastard had told her no man would touch her with a ten-foot pole if she asked for the sort of things she actually dreamed of in the bedroom—being bitten and choked, being bound and used, being praised and degraded, and so much more. But was that true? She'd only had one other serious relationship besides Sebastian, and that was in her early twenties. She'd changed since then. Was she really that different from other women?

After being humiliated enough to seek refuge in this little town, it was time to take control. She needed to get back in touch with herself and work out what a healthy relationship should be like. Especially after Sebastian had left such a bitter taste in her mouth.

She needed to rebuild her spirit so she could return home and be strong enough to leave Sebastian for good. They'd never officially broken up before, but he'd come back. He always came back. No matter how terrible the fight. No matter how many times he called her worthless. He always managed to manipulate her into forgiving him.

Not this time.

Two years and this was how it ended. What a joke. How it took this long to leave him, she'd never fully understand. They say it's hard to leave the cycle of abuse once you're in it. But he never really abused her. Did he? Thinking about her longest relationship in that context was unsettling. But when she examined their dynamic closer, the yelling, fighting, talking down to her, slowly cutting her off from her friends and hobbies…it seemed that way. Her best friends, Brittany and Layla, had tried to warn her, but she couldn't see past the charming man he was at the start of their relationship. He'd manipulated and isolated her. In truth, he'd intimidated her at times. It certainly wasn't a healthy relationship.

But she didn't want to give him any more space in her mind.

She had a plan. Stay away from Sebastian for ten days, and figure out what *she* wanted. For herself and in a relationship. Then she could go back to Ottawa and not crumble to Sebastian when he inevitably knocked at her door.

So what did she want in a partner? Roman and his insane body came to mind. Though she needed more than physical attraction. Would he even be interested in her if he knew what she was into sexually? She shook her head. That was Sebastian talking, not her.

Roman seemed supportive at the pub earlier in the day, although she hadn't gone into any type of detail. Instead, she glossed over the whole situation, enough to give him the gist. And she certainly didn't play the voice message for him. That was way too personal. He'd be running for the hills.

On the other hand, he called Sebastian a coward for not listening to her needs. Perhaps that meant he was open to listening to a partner's preferences. But she was getting ahead of herself. The priority wasn't to bang the hot pub owner, who also owned the most beautiful bed and breakfast she'd ever seen.

She scooted off the bed, unzipped her suitcase, and began unpacking her clothes. The dresser in the corner was more than large enough to hold all her stuff. While she was at it, she decided to change into something more comfortable. She tugged on her black knee socks, an oversized white t-shirt, and the booty shorts she'd been wearing as pajamas for the past three years.

Unpacked and snug in her slouchy clothes, she heaved the duvet off the king-sized bed and dragged it to the snuggle chair. She curled up in the nest of pillows and reclined.

She felt better than she had at the beginning of the day. Taking time to explore what she wanted, not what Sebastian told her she should want, sounded freeing. In a week and a half, she hoped to return to Ottawa a woman confident in what she wanted. A woman she could be proud of.

Chapter Four

LOGAN

Roman was standing in the kitchen with a big, dumb grin plastered on his face. No doubt the woman he'd brought home was the cause of said big, dumb grin.

Logan wouldn't get mad. That wouldn't help the situation. Though it was hard to get mad when his best friend appeared so delighted. He simply needed to explain to Roman why having someone living with them for ten days would not be beneficial when they were on a strict timeline to finish the guest suites. Three and a half months. That's all the time they had left. He needed to make Roman see reason.

Setting the pizza on the kitchen counter, he crossed his arms and opened his mouth to speak. Roman cut him off before he could.

"Before you say anything, Logey," Roman said, "you said this was fine when I called you. You can't change your mind now."

A headache was already forming behind his eyes. Logan pinched the bridge of his nose. "You didn't leave me much of a choice, Banks. What did you say? That she would be *sleeping on the street tonight* if I didn't agree to let her stay?"

At least Roman had the decency to look sheepish. Logan knew it wouldn't last.

"And was that remotely true?" he demanded.

Roman ran his fingers through his beard. "Gertie's fully booked at the hotel and was going to call the ladies in her mahjong group to see if Ava could sleep on one of their couches. Their couches, Logan!"

He scowled. "And a couch isn't good enough for this Ava?"

"I seriously think she would've found a bench outside the pub and slept there tonight. So a couch would have been fine." Roman crossed his arms in a challenge.

"And so you offered our place…why?"

"Because it was the right thing to do. We have the space, and she needs it. It also wouldn't hurt to make some extra cash. And if she leaves a good review once we're officially open, that would be good for business." Roman took a long swig of his beer, evidently satisfied with his argument.

He was silent. How could he object to that? It'd

basically be like refusing a guest who booked a stay at their B&B.

"Listen, her asswipe of an ex-boyfriend sent out her very private information in a voice message to her entire contact list. She was so mortified, she left town."

Logan narrowed his eyes. "What kind of private information? People don't skip out on their life because someone blasts their social insurance number to their contact list."

"Private sexual information, Logan. To her family, her colleagues, her boss, for fuck's sake."

He took a deep breath and held it for a beat before exhaling. Not what he expected. "The guy sounds like a real piece of work."

Roman grunted his agreement.

"Fine. We'll talk about this later." Logan needed to decompress. He couldn't do that with his stomach growling and Roman in his ear. His best friend always was the one to jump to the aid of others. He should know. A quality he normally admired, even if it annoyed him at times.

Logan preferred for people to learn how to take care of themselves, then do things the right way the next time. If this woman didn't make proper plans, then that was on her. It shouldn't be on them to make everything better. But that's what Roman did. Really, he shouldn't expect anything different.

"Fine, but we will talk about it." Roman stared

him right in the eyes, waiting for confirmation from him.

Logan nodded sharply and shifted his attention to the pepperoni pizza in front of him. Starving, he wasn't going to wait any longer to dig in. Yes, they would talk about it later.

"Pizza's here!" Roman called up the stairs.

Logan shook his head. If Roman had any sense, he'd go to Ava's room and tell her in a normal fashion. Knock on her door, show her some respect. But Roman was impulsive and a bit like a puppy in the way he got so excited about things. Hollering up the stairs was a perfectly fine way to invite a guest to dinner.

"You don't want to go get her?"

Roman shrugged. "She said I could just yell at her when the food arrived."

"This should be good," Logan said to himself, taking a seat on one of the bar stools tucked under the counter.

Light footsteps traipsed down the stairs and a head full of bouncy blonde curls appeared. Followed by long, lithe legs that led to a sinfully short pair of bottoms which perfectly accentuated her ass. A spray of freckles dotted her pink cheeks. And those thick, dark eyelashes…

Fuck.

Now he knew why Roman had jumped at the chance to give her a place to stay.

Ava was sexy as hell.

ROMAN

He watched as Ava's gaze landed on Logan, taking in his closed off body language. She approached cautiously, but with a smile. "Hey, thank you so much for letting me stay here. I really appreciate it. I'm Ava," she said, holding out a hand to Logan.

He accepted her outstretched palm and gave a curt shake. "Logan."

Roman rolled his eyes. Always the charmer. He handed Ava a plate and gestured for her to dig in.

"Hawaiian! My favourite." Ava's eyes twinkled as she took in the sight of the extra-large pizza sitting on the counter.

Logan scoffed around a bite of pepperoni, and Roman couldn't help but grin. He had a feeling Ava would be a fan of ham and pineapple, like him. Logan hated the flavour and maintained that it was the lowest of the low for pizza toppings. Not very Canadian of him, in Roman's opinion. But Logan always bought it for him anyway.

Roman took the opportunity to touch her on the shoulder. "I knew you had good taste."

She piled two slices on her plate and took a seat next to Logan at the counter.

"How long are you planning to stay here, exactly?" Logan asked, an icy bite in his tone.

Ava glanced nervously between the two of them, then down at her plate. Shit. He didn't want her to feel uncomfortable.

"As long as she needs," Roman interjected, crossing his arms.

"We have a lot of work to do to get this place up-and-running in the next three and a half months. Installing the plumbing, tiling the showers, painting the suites, buying more furniture, marketing, advertising, and…do I need to go on?"

"I promise I won't be a bother. I'll stay out of your way," Ava said earnestly. No doubt trying to quell the palpable annoyance radiating off of Logan.

"You're not a bother, Ava. Logan's just very particular, like I said. It takes a special type of person to see past his bonehead exterior," Roman joked, sending a look Logan's way that said 'lighten up.'

Logan scowled at him.

"I can eat in my room, if you'd like?" Ava offered, as if she didn't want to rock Logan's boat any further.

"That's unnecessary, love. He'll play nice. Won't you, Logan?" Roman couldn't have given a more pointed stare if he tried. His idiot best friend was going to ruin this for him.

"I'd rather not. Off you go." Logan gestured toward the staircase.

"Not a problem at all. I don't want to be a

nuisance." Ava grabbed her plate and a nearby napkin, then rose from her seat. "Have a good night, and thank you both again."

The sound of her door clicking shut followed a few moments later.

Roman swatted his friend hard across the shoulder.

"What?" Logan cried out.

"You know what, you asshole. Why do you always have to be Mr. Surly? Is that how you're going to treat all the guests we have?"

"We have things to do, and she'll be in the way."

"You know that's not true."

"So you won't spend the entire time she's here trying to fuck her?"

"No." Shit. He said that a little too quickly.

"Yeah, that's what I thought."

"I like her. She's cute, she's friendly, and she's easy to talk to."

"You've known her for one day." Logan raised an eyebrow. "Don't tell me you're already head over heels for the new girl in town."

"And if I am?"

Logan's lips pressed together tightly while he contemplated the situation. "She can stay the night," he huffed. "In the morning, we can work out alternate plans. We need to finish this place by January. We can't fall behind because your dick liked what it saw."

"Tell me yours doesn't and I'll make her leave right now."

No reply.

"Exactly."

Logan finished his last slice of pepperoni pizza and stalked off to his room.

The sense of victory that settled in Roman's mind was quickly replaced by a small worry: If Logan found Ava attractive too, what did that mean for him?

He knew Logan would never purposely interfere with a woman he was interested in, but he couldn't help but wonder what made Logan change his mind so quickly from letting Ava stay, to advocating for her to leave. She'd done nothing to him personally. Maybe he really was worried about keeping it in his pants. That would be a first.

If Logan wanted something, it wasn't often that he couldn't have it. Roman would need to make it clear that he was interested in Ava, and that was that.

Shit, that made him seem like a caveman staking his claim or something. But it was how he felt. If Ava was in town for ten days, he had a short time to get to know her and possibly win her over.

He prayed Logan wouldn't stand in his way.

LOGAN

Morning came too fast. Normally, he had no problem waking by six. But last night, he tossed and turned, thoughts of Ava roaming free in his mind. How her wild, curly hair bounced as she walked into the kitchen. The tiny shorts that barely covered her ass. And, God—those knee-high socks she had on. What kind of outfit was that? Was she trying to give him a heart attack?

No. Not him.

Roman.

She met Roman first.

His rotten fucking luck that his best friend saw Ava first. And worse—he seemed to really like her after only half a day. So any chance he had to be with Ava in any capacity was out the window. Not that he was searching for a relationship.

He wanted someone to fuck. And Ava was stunning. Plus, she appeared confident in her skin. The way she bounded down the stairs in those tiny shorts, not concerned in the slightest that her ass was half on display for two strangers. The confidence in her body spoke to him, as did the quick way she complied when he told her off. It made him wonder if she'd comply as easily with his requests in the bedroom, too.

He wanted to think if he ran into her on Main Street, and she needed a place to stay, that he would've offered. But when it came right down to it, he knew he wouldn't have. That just wasn't him. If anything, he would've flirted, brought her here for a quick and dirty time together, then charged her for a room.

Things were better that way. There was a reason he kept his walls up. And he'd been through enough therapy to know he was difficult. But he also knew that the people who mattered were the people who stayed. Stuck by his side through thick and thin. Put in the effort to get through to him. Like Roman.

Shaking off the lack of sleep, Logan rose to do his morning routine. Get rid of the five o'clock shadow, have a quick shower, apply moisturizer, brush his teeth, and make sure each product went right back where it belonged on his sink counter. A bit of cologne and he was ready.

He needed to talk to Ava before Roman got up and became her tough protector again. They were busy. They had rooms to paint, bathrooms to tile, furniture to pick out. There was no time to play host to a girl looking for a handout. He'd make her see reason. Gertie would find a place for her to stay, like originally offered, before Roman called him from the pub.

Logan went upstairs to the guest rooms and knocked on Ava's door. She'd probably be sleeping, but that was too bad. Time to get moving and be on her way.

The door flew open and left Logan gawking at the sight before him.

Ava gave the impression she'd been awake for a while. Her hair was thrown back in a messy ponytail high on her head, the oversized t-shirt she had on the night before was speckled with what appeared to be… mortar? And did she have a bit on her cheek and hands as well? What the hell was this girl doing?

"Morning," she said, forcing a smile that didn't quite meet her eyes.

"Uh, morning," he replied, completely thrown for a loop.

"How can I help you, Logan?" Her voice was sweet and polite, no doubt doing her best to win him over so he would let her stay longer.

"We need to talk. I think it's best if we find you another place to—" He cut himself off, unable to concentrate, not knowing what she'd been doing before he knocked on her door. "Why are you covered in mortar? What have you been doing in here?" He stepped into the room, not bothering to ask if he could enter. He built the place, after all.

"Oh, well…" Her gaze fell to her feet, then rose to him. "You said you didn't want me getting in the way or slowing your progress down, so I figured in addition to paying for the room here, I would help out as well."

"Help how?"

"Come," she said, taking his hand and pulling him toward the ensuite bathroom. "I'll show you."

He slipped his hand out of hers and didn't miss the small expression of hurt that crossed her face. She recovered quickly, though. Logan was surprised he even saw it.

"Ta-da!" She stood by the washroom door, holding her arms out.

His jaw dropped. "You tiled the shower?" Disbelief overtook him and he couldn't do anything else but stare.

"I couldn't sleep. So at three o'clock this morning, I decided to make myself useful. The tiles were already cut and the other supplies were lying around. Easy as pie." She shrugged her shoulders like working through the night was no big deal.

"Where did you learn to do this?"

"My dad's a contractor. I grew up helping him with stuff like this. Tiling a bathroom is child's play," she stated matter-of-factly, but the glint in her eye told him she was proud of her handiwork.

"Next time, ask before you do something like this." He didn't bother keeping the bitterness out of his tone. For the life of him, he couldn't be polite.

She was stunning, willing to work, and knew her way around a trowel? His. Fucking. Luck.

Ava frowned at his reaction. "What?"

He needed to get her out of here. "I don't need you botching our plans and putting us behind." He took a step closer to her. So close, his chest almost brushed against her own. "Stay out of our way."

Her head tipped up so she could meet his eyes. A flash of defiance flitted through them. "I'm pretty sure Roman wants me to *get in his way*."

Another step closer. She was pressed against the door and his body was flush with hers. Placing his arms on either side of her head, he boxed her in. "I think he just wants to get *in* you," he rumbled out, low and throaty.

"Looks like you might want that, too." Her gaze drifted down to where their bodies were pressed together.

He was definitely sporting a semi.

"See something you like?" he taunted.

"Are you always this much of an asshole?" Her chest rapidly rose and fell. A sweet crimson blush climbed her neck.

Damn, he wanted to lick it off her peachy little face.

"Always," he growled in her ear. Dropping his arms, he stepped away, and she scooted to the open space of the bedroom.

"I'd like you to leave now."

"I feel the same way, sweetheart." He sauntered out the door and down the steps, hoping that when he next saw her, she'd have her suitcase in hand, requesting Roman give her a ride in town.

Chapter Five

AVA

"He did what?" Roman bellowed, pacing in the kitchen. "I'm gonna need to have a serious talk with him."

"Please, don't." Ava grasped his big, tattooed arm, stopping him in his tracks. "Logan's obviously upset I'm in his space. I can understand that. He doesn't need to be such a dick about it, but…" She sighed, rubbing her temples. What did she know? Maybe he was bad with strangers. Maybe it took him a long time to warm up to new faces. Maybe there was something about her that set him off. Cutting him some slack was the least she could do.

"Ava. It's not okay that he said those things. I only want to *get in you?* You tiled the entire shower last night, for Christ's sake! He should say thank you, not try to upset you." He ran his fingers hastily through his long brown locks, shoving it out of his eyes, before quickly throwing it into a bun.

The gesture made her heart race.

"I'll talk to him as soon as he returns from picking up paint for the guest rooms." Roman glared at the foyer of the B&B.

She'd heard the front door slam after their conflict in the bathroom. What was that all about, anyway?

"Let's take a bit of time to cool off first, okay?" The last thing she wanted was another heated confrontation between these two—or her and Logan. Though she knew Roman would defend her, even if Logan was his best friend.

How these two were friends didn't make sense to her. They seemed to be complete opposites. Roman was sweet and thoughtful, willing to help a total stranger. Logan was sour and rude, wanting to kick her out the second he laid eyes on her. If Roman liked Logan, there must be something hidden behind the scowl on his pretty face.

And, God, what a pretty face it was. Yesterday, a five o'clock shadow accentuated his sharp jawline perfectly. She noticed it missing this morning. His dirty blonde hair edged on brunette and was short and swept back from his fair face in a stylish cut. Even the permanent scowl on his sun-kissed face did nothing to detract from his movie star features.

Though they couldn't be more opposite, she

hoped to get to know them both better during the coming days.

Roman took a deep breath in through his mouth and exhaled slowly out his nose. "Okay. It's no use talking to him when I'm all wound up. What do you say we head into town and I'll show you around? We'll make ourselves scarce for when Logan returns."

There was definitely more to Logan's behaviour than her being here. That much she knew. She was a sexually repressed thirty-three-year-old with an asshat narcissist for an ex-boyfriend, so she knew emotional baggage when she saw it.

"I'd love that. Let's go." She wrapped her arm around his. "Wait—I need my purse."

He set his hand on her arm. "This trip's on me, love."

Her instinct was to protest, but she had a feeling Roman wouldn't let her argue. She nodded, and they walked outside, arm-in-arm.

After a quick ten-minute ride in his pickup, they pulled onto Main Street and parked at the beginning of the strip.

"Where should we begin?" She was curious to explore and see what the little town had to offer.

"How about right here at Wakin' & Bacon?" He pointed to the little café they currently stood by. "I figured we'd get coffee and a bite to eat, then mosey down the road. We can duck into whatever stores pique your interest."

She smiled. Names like Wakin' & Bacon definitely added to the small town's charm. "I love that idea."

Roman held open the door, and she stepped inside. Freshly brewed coffee was the first scent to hit her, followed closely by cinnamon, syrup, and, of course, bacon.

"Do you trust me?" His voice rumbled from directly behind her.

When his arm rested lightly around her waist, his palm on her hip, butterflies danced around her stomach in a frenzy. She managed to nod.

"Good."

Leaving her side, he went to the counter and ordered two drinks and sandwiches, both to go. She saw him smile at the dark-haired cashier and chat with her like they were old friends. The charm dripped off him effortlessly. If she was a betting woman, she'd bet that Roman was the town sweetheart. The guy everyone loved and could rely on. That was the kind of energy he exuded.

"Alright, I took a guess," Roman announced, carrying over two to-go cups of what she figured was coffee. "Please tell me you like your coffee hot and sickly sweet?"

Her eyebrows shot up as she reached out to take the cup. "How did you know that?"

"Had a feeling." He shrugged one shoulder and gave her an impish smile. "Maria is the owner. She and her family moved here from Argentina fifteen years ago. The batch of dulce de leche she makes each week is to die for. She uses it in her alfajores and as a filling for her cinnamon sugar muffins."

Her mouth began to water, and she did her best not to drool on the café floor.

"But I asked her to add a scoop to your latte. Try it."

Swirling her cup with a few circles of her wrist, the drink's aroma wafted up and made her eyes roll back in her head. It smelled like a cup of heaven. Literal heaven. She took a sip, not caring that the coffee was piping hot, and let the flavours mingle on her tongue.

"Oh. My. God," she moaned. This might very well be the best latte ever.

"I'm pretty sure that sound means you like it." Roman winked, sending her butterflies into another tizzy. "And here are our sandwiches." Roman grabbed two foil-wrapped packages and thanked the cashier, who she guessed was Maria.

She called out her own thank you, gave her a wave, and followed Roman out the door.

Taking the mystery item from him, she unwrapped the top half and stared at it. Nothing prepared her for what was between the two English muffins. "Is that…grape jelly?"

"Oh yeah." Roman grinned, already tearing into his sandwich. "Peanut butter and jelly with smoked bacon and a sunny-side-up egg."

"You like this?" she asked in disbelief.

"Nope. I *love* this. I begged Maria to make it for me so often, she eventually added it to the menu. Now it's one of the most popular breakfast sandwiches at the joint."

Her skepticism must've shown on her face, because Roman lit up with a hearty chuckle and waggled the sandwich in his hand.

"Come on, have a bite. You liked the coffee, right?"

That was true. Time to live a little. Ava took a big mouthful and bit down. The hot yolk burst on her tongue and mixed with the salt of the bacon and peanut butter. The sweetness of the grape jelly rounded everything off. Roman was one hundred percent right.

"You win," she admitted. "This is fantastic. I'm trying my hardest not to moan again."

"Don't let me stop you." That wicked grin had returned. He took another bite and licked a smear of peanut butter off his thick forefinger.

If she was in danger of moaning before, she was on high alert now. That tongue on those tattooed fingers. Yup, it did things to her. And he knew it.

They strolled down Main Street, taking in the sights. Not that there was a lot to see, but there were many cute shops. Roman bought her a shaker of delicious smelling Cajun seasoning at Paprika and Co. as well as a fancy can of cream soda at a specialty candy store called The Sugar Buffet.

But her favourite, by far, was the corner drugstore that also doubled as a sweets shop. It didn't have a fancy pun for a name and the façade was unassuming, yet Dean's Drug Mart was the most interesting store in the little town.

It had the regular stock of a drugstore, but also sold beautifully arranged succulent planters, vinyl records, and an array of art prints. At the counter was a large glass case filled with twenty varieties of handmade chocolates that were all the same shape but with different colours and flavours.

She pursued the display. "I'd love to buy Gertie a gift for being so wonderful to me. Do you think she'd like chocolates?"

"She's actually a lover of anything maple. Get her a jar of this." He handed her a container of maple butter from a nearby shelf. "It's made at Mapleside Sugar Bush, just a few hours east of here. Don't tell her I said this, but she goes through a jar a week." He tapped the top of the jar in her hands.

Ava grinned. "Thanks for the insider information." She made her way to the till but stopped short. "Shit. I don't have my purse. Do you mind? I'll pay you back when we get to the B&B."

"Not a problem, love. Pick out something for yourself, as well. On me."

She lifted her hands in protest. “Oh, thank you, but I’m set. You’ve already done so much for me.”

“I’ll take one of each,” Roman said to the man behind the counter, pointing to the chocolates. “And the jar of maple butter.”

He paid for the treats and escorted her out the door.

She felt her cheeks turn pink as she smiled. “You didn’t have to do that, Roman.”

He simply shrugged his shoulders and said, “I know you have a sweet tooth.”

She could get used to this. A man who is kind and giving? Who pays attention to the little things? Definitely three things she mentally added to her list of desirable traits in a partner.

Ava placed her hand on his forearm. “Thank you. Would it be okay if I ran into Gertie’s hotel to deliver the butter?”

“Go for it. I’ll wait for you right here.” He leaned casually against the outside of Dean’s Drug Mart. It should’ve been illegal to make leaning against a wall so sexy.

Ava ducked into The Quiet Shore Hotel a few doors down and found Gertie setting out butter tarts by the coffee machine in the lobby. Judging by the rich smell of pastry and caramel, they were freshly baked. Violet tassels hung from her ears today, along with a matching statement piece around her neck. She always seemed to have the nicest jewellery.

Gertie beamed when she saw her. "Ava! So nice of you to drop in, dear."

"I brought you a little something to say thank you for your hospitality yesterday." She held out the jar of maple butter. "A little birdy told me you loved maple."

Gertie joined her and accepted the gift. "Would that birdy's name be Roman, by chance?"

She laughed. "That obvious?"

Gertie tilted her head. "He's been buying me maple-flavoured candies and treats for as long as I can remember. I don't have the heart to tell him I don't care for the flavour," she tittered.

Ava gasped. "You don't like maple?"

Gertie was full-on snorting now. "I know, what kind of Canadian am I?"

"I need to get you something else, then. Roman was so confident that you'd love this." She motioned for Gertie to return the butter.

"Oh, no you don't." She clutched the gift to her chest. "Roman can never know. I don't have the heart to tell him. Besides, I set out the fudge or chocolates he brings me for the guests. Or I bake tarts and pastries using the maple butter and serve it as our continental breakfast. Nothing goes to waste."

She admired the woman more each time they spoke. "Your secret's safe with me, Gertie. I promise."

Walking down the opposite side of the street toward where the truck was parked, her eyes were trained on Roman.

"What? Do I have peanut butter on my face or something?" Crossing his eyes to see his beard, he wiped at it in a broad, exaggerated motion.

A heartfelt laugh poured out of her. "No, I'm just admiring the view," she admitted.

"Like what you see?" He grinned, slinging his arm around her shoulders and letting it rest there.

"I think I might," she said, popping a chocolate he'd bought her into her mouth.

And that was the truth. She'd only known him for a day and a half, but she liked him. He was funny, generous, and thoughtful. When she needed help, he jumped at the chance to provide it. She was pretty sure he was successful—owning both a pub and a construction business. All things she definitely wished for in a man. Oh, and it didn't hurt that he looked like a god of war with those tattoos and long hair. Not to mention being built like a brick house.

"I need to pick up some furniture for the guest bedrooms and balconies. You feel like taking a detour with me?"

"I've got nothing but time right now, Roman. Take me wherever you need to go." She leaned into him slightly, testing how he felt next to her.

His arm was warm and solid against her shoulders.

The whole thing was too good to be true. She came here to get away from her idiot ex-boyfriend, not to lust after the hunky B&B owner. But Roman was swiftly showing her how a real man behaved. She couldn't get involved with someone right after a breakup, could she?

That would be dumb. Irresponsible. But oh so good…

Though it wouldn't work long-term. Roman's life was in Little Greenfield, and hers wasn't. She had a career she worked hard for in Ottawa. An apartment. Friends. Well, estranged friends. But maybe she could reach out and start mending those relationships now that she was done with Sebastian.

And who was to say Roman was trustworthy in regards to the heart? Sure, coffee, breakfast sandwiches, and chocolates were marvellous things, but to trust someone with private pieces of you was a different matter.

She'd trusted Sebastian. In hindsight, there were definite red flags that she now saw a lot clearer. Although she sensed that Roman was different. His reaction to her abridged version of events with Sebastian was not what she expected, and he oozed confidence. Maybe sharing the details of what happened wouldn't scare him away.

When they got to his truck, she reached for the passenger door handle, but Roman closed in behind her and gently put his hand over hers, stilling her. The touch sent fire through her from head to toe.

"Forgive me for being forward." His tone ran like warm honey down her back. "But I've been thinking about your lips all morning. I'd really like to kiss you."

She spun to look at him and instantly melted. The need in his eyes sang to her soul. Any thought of not getting involved with him evaporated like water on a scorching summer day.

He pushed her curls back and cupped her face. "Would that be alright?"

She managed to nod. Of course kissing her would be alright. More than alright. His strong hand against her cheek and the desire in his dark eyes called to her.

Roman slowly took a step closer, pressing her against the truck's door as he cradled her head. He didn't rush as he tipped her face up to meet his kiss.

The moment their lips met, a sigh left him. As if he'd been waiting on bated breath for the taste of her and could now finally breathe.

Unhurried at first, his tongue swept over the seam of her lips, and she opened easily for him. His arm wrapped around her waist, and he held her close. Their mouths moved with each other in a familiar way, like they'd done this before. Softly, they explored. Her fingers climbed his broad chest, relishing his hard muscles. So strong, yet so gentle.

A whimper left her lips and Roman deepened the kiss, devouring her with a gravelly sound of approval.

The way he kissed her felt like he owned her body. He invaded and overwhelmed her senses.

He ran his palm down her thigh and lifted her leg around his hips, grinding himself against her.

Ava's head dropped against the truck. Even through his jeans, the brush of his hard cock sent shivers straight to her pussy. Roman ran his tongue down her neck, ending with a nip on her shoulder.

"You taste so good, love," he rasped.

She clutched the nape of his neck, urging him to bite again. Harder.

But Roman drew back until his forehead rested on hers. His heaving chest mirrored hers, both breathless and wanting. His palm rested on her ass, hovering dangerously close to somewhere else she'd like him to touch.

"Why'd you stop?" she whispered.

He shook his head. "Because I'm pretty sure what comes next will be considered public indecency."

She laughed, and he kissed her one more time. His skill for turning her on and diffusing the tension at the same time was a true talent. She was more comfortable with him in a day and a half than she'd been with Sebastian after two years.

He nudged her sideways and opened the truck door. "Hop in, love."

As soon as she was seated, he closed the door for her. Always a gentleman. Sliding in behind the wheel, he threw the truck in gear and headed down the road that led out of town.

Oh, yes. She definitely wanted to hook-up with Roman and experience the freedom of being with a new partner. Screw being fresh off a breakup. He'd already demonstrated several admirable traits and treated her like she was worth something. She simply had to summon the nerve to ask him. A kiss was one thing, requesting kink-laced sex was another.

But she was going to make the most of her time in Little Greenfield, and that involved delving inward and deciding what she wanted for a change. No one to tell her what to do or how to act. And if she wanted to pursue Roman in any sort of way, she could. She was single, after all.

If he was truly a good man, this could be something real. They'd work out the details later. The thought filled her with both hope and apprehension. She didn't intend to find a partner on this poorly planned getaway, or so soon after leaving Sebastian, but she decided to keep her heart open to the possibility.

LOGAN

By the time Logan returned from buying supplies to finish painting the guest rooms, Roman's truck was gone. He hadn't had a chance to speak with Roman before he left for the large hardware store two towns over, but he hoped to God that Roman had taken Ava to stay somewhere else.

Logan gathered the brushes, tape, another drop cloth, and paint tray and climbed the stairs to the guest level. When he entered Ava's room, his face fell and he let a string of curses fly. Her suitcase remained beside the bed. The little shorts she'd worn last night were tossed casually on the mattress beside her oversized t-shirt. And was that a—? Oh, for fuck's sake. It was. A lacy pink thong was on the floor.

That was absolutely the last thing he needed to be picturing her in. The knee-high socks were already seared into his brain. Knowing that tiny scrap of fabric was on her pussy—that was too much.

He could handle it. Ava and her things were not going to distract him. He busied himself taping around baseboards and windows, laying out the drop cloths, and getting everything else he needed in order. When he was ready, he started painting the room the deep olive colour he and Roman picked out a few weeks ago, doing his best to ignore the sinful scrap of fabric on the floor.

His brows furrowed, and he shifted his dick in his jeans. Didn't the stupid thing know he was annoyed, not horny? Why did he have to have such a thing for skimpy underwear?

The pink lace called to him. He tried to ignore it.

He wasn't a hormonal teenage boy anymore. But the thong remained in the forefront of his mind. After painting half the room, he couldn't stand it anymore. He snagged it off the floor and shoved it in his pocket. No one had to know. She would think they were misplaced, and he'd have a tiny piece of Ava since Roman already laid claim to her.

It wasn't like he wanted to be with her, anyway. But few visitors came to Little Greenfield—especially not women their age—and damn if he couldn't use a hot, dirty fuck. Though Ava didn't strike him as the type who'd be into that. It didn't stop him from picturing her writhing underneath him, calling out his name. He was sure he could convince her, given the chance.

Fuck. He did want to be with her.

He shook his head to clear his mind. Roman saw her first. Fair's fair. He had to get her out of the B&B. It wasn't so much about falling behind on the work as not being able to stand being in the same room as her. The instant she bounced down those stairs and into the kitchen, he was done. He cursed himself for telling Roman having a guest stay a few nights was fine, since he artfully neglected to tell him just what *kind* of guest would be staying with them.

Everything about her screamed *his type*. Her long curly hair, the confidence in her walk, and the innocence in her eyes. Especially her eyes. He wanted to change them from naïve to knowing. The things he would do to her.

He wanted to ruin her in the best way possible. See the mascara running down her face. Hear her choke on his cock. Watch her body tremble at his touch.

His dumb-fucking-luck that she wandered into The White Pine Pub and met Roman.

Not that it was his best friend's fault. It wasn't like he planned for this to happen. Roman would never do anything to hurt him, he knew that. No question. And possibly wanting to pursue a relationship won out over whatever he was feeling, anyway. Roman was antsy, always telling him how he wanted to take the next step in life, but he hadn't found the right woman.

Logan wiped his brow with his knuckles and surveyed his work. Everything was painted, appeared even, and he was happy with the outcome. He transferred the supplies to the next guest suite. Once the paint was dry, he'd return to remove the tape from the baseboards and along the ceiling. Continued alone time doing repetitive work was what he needed to clear his head.

But his thoughts kept returning to Ava. It wasn't out of the realm of possibility that Ava was the right woman for Roman. She hadn't been in town for long, but stranger things had happened.

Logan's parents dated for two years, were engaged for another year and a half, and still proceeded to get divorced when he was eight. Roman's parents had a whirlwind romance that lasted four weeks before they eloped to Vegas. Now they were going on something like thirty-seven years of marriage.

So who was he to stand in the way of Roman's potential happiness? He needed to tone down his assholery and be a decent friend. At least he would try.

Ducking into Ava's room one final time to remove the last can of paint, he noticed her purse on the bedside table. Her phone peeked out the top. What did Roman say last night? The reason she was here was because of a voice message from her ex?

He plucked the phone out of the bag. No password. Oh, Ava. So trusting. Especially after being burned by her ex.

Scrolling through her messages, he clicked in and out of any with a man's name. Finally, he landed on Sebastian. The last message from him was a voice recording that was four minutes and twenty-seven seconds long. Prick.

He quickly forwarded it to himself, then deleted the proof that he'd done so. He couldn't let her know he'd invaded her privacy. That wouldn't win him any points. But if the message was bad enough to make her abandon her home to hide out in Little Greenfield, he needed to know what it said.

Tucking Ava's phone back where he found it, he grabbed the paint can and exited the room. The lock on the front door clicked, signaling that Roman had returned, and he heard it swing open with its distinctive woosh. Roman's deep baritone and Ava's giggle floated up to the guest suites where he stood.

Perfect timing.

Chapter Six

ROMAN

Who knew picking out patio furniture would be so enjoyable? They drove into Huntsville, the biggest town within day-trip distance, and spent the afternoon hunting down the perfect furniture at second-hand stores and vintage shops.

Ava found a well-loved wooden set for her room's balcony. A cafe table and a pair of loungers, perfect for two. The stain was worn, and needed a refresh, but they suited the B&B perfectly. Roman had picked out some cushioned bistro furniture, nothing fancy. A couple of chairs and tables for the other two decks.

Roman carried the loungers to her room, and Ava trailed close behind with the little table. He was ribbing her about taking such a small load when Logan appeared at the top of the stairs.

"Roman. Ava." He nodded.

They didn't get a chance to talk earlier this morning, so Roman figured the best approach was to be cautious. "Hey, bud. What've you been doing while we were gone?"

"I finished painting Ava's guest suite. The fumes might be strong. Fair warning."

Ava nodded, acknowledging his statement, but kept quiet. She took a step closer to Roman, and he puffed out his chest. Being her safe place was a good feeling.

Logan's gaze locked on Ava, and he took a breath before saying, "Listen, Ava can stay. She did a decent job tiling the shower. If she helps us out and leaves a good review, then it's a win-win situation. Deal?"

"Deal," she answered, without hesitation.

Roman breathed a sigh of relief. "We picked out fantastic chairs and tables for the balconies. The rest are in the back of the truck if you want to help bring them up."

Logan gave a curt nod and took the stairs two at a time while Roman continued with Ava to her balcony. Thank goodness Logan had come around. Having a come-to-Jesus talk about his abhorrent actions wasn't something Roman wanted to do today. Nonetheless, he'd have to knock him on the head for what he said to Ava, but they were moving in the right direction.

Sometimes his friend needed time to think. Though he wasn't sure what he needed to think about, per se. When he called to ask if a stranded visitor could crash at their place for a while, he was mostly amenable. Sure, it took a bit of convincing, but that's how Logan was. A sourpuss who eventually saw the light with a little help.

No, it wasn't until Logan saw Ava yesterday that his attitude changed. Something about the situation bothered his best friend, and he would make it his mission to find out.

"How's this?" Roman asked after arranging the two loungers to overlook the pine trees behind the building.

"I love it," Ava said, setting the table between them. "Now I just need a cup of tea, a book, and I could lounge here for hours."

"Let me get you some."

"Oh, I didn't mean right now. There's still plenty to do."

"Take a break for half an hour, I insist. You want Earl Grey? Herbal? Matcha?"

She grinned. "If you *insist*. Earl Grey, please and thank you. And I'll get you that five bucks for the maple butter."

Roman liked this girl. A lot. Sure, they'd only spent a day and a half together at this point, but she radiated an energy that spoke to him. She was easy to talk to. He didn't find there were any awkward moments together. And their chemistry was through the roof. Was this what a soulmate felt like?

The heat in her eyes was the same as the heat in his. He'd made his attraction no secret. Any chance he got today, he'd touched her. An arm around her shoulder, a playful touch on her hand, a flirtatious whisper with his lips almost on her ear.

He jogged downstairs to the kitchen and put the kettle on. If Ava had given him any sign she wasn't interested, he'd have backed off. But she leaned in to his touches and grabbed his hand playfully when they walked through the stores. Her skin on his made his heart beat out of his chest. It was insane that another man let her go. Scratch that. It was insane that another man insulted her, humiliated her, and practically forced her to leave her home. If Roman was a different man, he might have a mind to track down Sebastian and teach him a lesson.

But he was a lover, not a fighter.

Logan was the fighter. He was slightly taller than Roman, with a more athletic build compared to his own broad frame, and the anger inside fueled Logan. That rage was a scary thing to behold when Logan directed it at someone specific. That didn't happen often. In fact, Roman had seen it no more than twice in their eighteen years as friends.

Once, when Logan's dad breezed into town unannounced and tried to make a half-assed apology for treating Logan like shit growing up. And once when an idiot was speeding down Main Street in his car and almost hit a kid on her bike. Both times, Logan chewed those men up and spit them out.

He sagged against the nearest kitchen cabinet. Thank goodness Ava could stay. They'd already discussed her helping put the finishing touches on the guest suites. When he'd asked if she wanted to finish tiling the rest of the showers, her eyes gleamed, obviously thrilled to be allowed to help.

Honestly, he didn't care if she lifted a finger. Roman just wanted her near. She made his heart race and his palms sweat. Not to mention his dick got a semi whenever she bent over to get something. Or whenever he thought about that damn kiss.

The entire drive home, Ava spouted off ideas about how she would help, drumming her fingers against his truck's windowpane. She'd tile the showers, tape the other two rooms to get them ready for painting, and bring them all beer after a long day of work. He loved watching the spark in her light up, especially after she arrived so dejected.

He poured the boiling water into a mug, added the tea bag, and snagged a fluffy blanket from the living area. He understood the time he'd spent with Ava was short, but something inside him screamed she was the person he'd been waiting for. All the time alone served a purpose. It brought her to him—forehead plastered on his bartop—and he wanted her to stay.

AVA

All things considered, Ava had a delightful day. Exploring Little Greenfield and picking out furniture in Huntsville with Roman was energizing. After getting the hell out of dodge, and landing in a place she'd never been before, she needed a day like this. A day to explore what life could be like away from Sebastian's control. The flirty touches and looks Roman gave her didn't hurt, either.

It's not like she didn't reciprocate. He was stupidly attractive and had a heart of gold. She'd be a fool not to, right? Not to mention that kiss was one of the best she'd had in a long time. Maybe ever.

She never thought she'd be interested in someone so quickly after the Sebastian debacle. There was a reason she was in Little Greenfield. And perhaps the sexy bar owner who was building his own bed and breakfast could help her discover what she actually wanted in a partner. If her desires were something worth fighting for, or if she should give in to the life she already knew.

Dispassionate, boring sex.

An ex-boyfriend who treated her like dirt.

The answer seemed obvious. But finding the mental and emotional strength to return home and say good riddance to Sebastian once and for all would be difficult. He constantly wormed his way into her life one way or another. She needed to experience life outside her bubble in Ottawa and outside of Sebastian's reach.

Tip-toeing down the staircase, she made her way to the guys' shared bathroom. Roman went to bed earlier, so she'd kept busy applying grout to the tiles she'd installed. Eager for a good scrub after making somewhat of a mess, she hoped the bathroom was free. No need for any unnecessary run-ins with Logan.

Even though he relented and said she could stay, she felt something was going on with him. Whether he still didn't want her there, found her annoying, or he didn't make friends quickly—something crawled up his ass the moment they'd met. How to get it out was a mystery.

When she entered the back part of the bed and breakfast, the first thing she noticed was the closed washroom door. Just her luck. She sidled closer and listened for running water or brushing teeth.

Nothing.

No sounds from within, but light spilled from beneath the door. Strange.

She tried the handle. Unlocked. She opened it slowly and took a tentative step inside.

"Don't you knock?" Logan asked disapprovingly, standing in front of the shower in nothing but his boxer briefs. His t-shirt and jeans lay in a pile at his feet.

"I'm so sorry!" She covered her eyes and spun around. "I didn't think anyone was in here."

"The door was shut, and the lights were on."

She pivoted her head slightly and peeked through her fingers. "I didn't hear anyone. I thought—"

"Were you hoping to catch me in the shower, Ava?" He raised his eyebrows and jutted his chin.

Her mouth opened and closed again. She had no words.

"If you wanted to see me naked, all you had to do was ask." His fingers slipped under the waistband of his underwear and tugged them down.

What was he doing? A flush climbed her neck. Yeah, this was happening. Her hands fell from her face, and she couldn't help but stare. Logan was getting naked in front of her while Roman slept down the hall. The ego on this man.

Shaking herself out of her stupor, she found her voice. "Does your superiority complex have no limits?"

"Why don't you come over here and ask me?" Gaze trained on her, it didn't falter for a second.

He was confident. She'd give him that. Though he had good reason to be. Despite not being as broad as Roman, his body was to die for. Lean and muscular. The kind of shape sculpted by manual labour. He was a smidge taller than Roman, too. His chest was clean shaven, but he kept a well-groomed treasure trail. And boy, did it lead to treasure.

Logan's dick was on full display.

Long. Thick. Well-groomed. Standing at full attention. Her gaze was glued to it. Why else would he take off his underwear in front of her? He wanted her to see it. And see it, she did.

Cocky son of a bitch.

"I'm waiting, Ava."

Steeling herself, she raised her head high and marched over to him, stopping mere inches away.

"Does. Your. Superiority. Complex. Have. No. Limits?"

Logan leaned in, his lips only a breath away from hers. "No."

Her heart was beating so fast, she was sure he could hear it. He was so close. All she had to do was angle her head, and they'd be kissing.

"Do what you need to do, then leave," he bit out.

The arrogance in his voice made her blood boil, but she couldn't deny how he made her feel. The evidence was painted across her body. Heated cheeks, sweaty palms, and rapid breathing. She wouldn't let him fluster her out of the washroom.

All she had to do was brush her teeth and wash her face, then get the hell out of here.

The squeak of the faucet drew her attention, and water pouring from the showerhead echoed in the room. Logan began lathering his body–completely visible behind the glass wall—with soap. She walked to her toiletries on Roman's sink, trying to keep her eyes trained on the mirror and away from Logan's gorgeous body. But not gawking at him was a herculean effort. She kept sneaking glances.

Brush, wash, get out.

Simple.

A hoarse groan cut the air. Her hands froze in the middle of splashing cold water on her face.

Another groan filled the room. Another.

Her gaze roamed to his form, and she took all of him in. Logan's legs were spread in a wide stance, one hand above his head, leaning on the glass wall. His other hand was wrapped around his cock, stroking.

Up, down.

Up, down.

Up, down.

His moaning was throaty and low. Seeing a man be so free with his body, with his pleasure, was hypnotizing. And so was him staring at her while he fucked his hand under the spray of hot water.

Holy hell.

If she thought he was sexy before, he was downright tempting now.

His mouth was open, and water flowed over every inch of him, highlighting the musculature of his body. Wet strands of hair hung in his face. His palm made a wicked noise as he pleasured himself to the sight of her.

"Ava."

She startled at his voice. Her name was on his

lips? Heat snaked around her belly, pooling inside her, begging to be unleashed.

"Look at me, Ava." Hunger filled his demand.

Her gaze connected with his and the lust there made her weak in the knees. The sounds emanating from Logan were crude, and watching him stroke himself was delicious.

Steam filled the shower, clouding the glass. He wiped it away so she would have an easier time watching. She drank in his physique, unable to tear herself away. Sweat beaded on her forehead, dripped down her chest. From the heat of the room or how aroused she was becoming, she didn't know.

"You like to watch?" he groaned out between strokes. "Or are you the one who wants to be watched?"

Oh, she wanted this. Wanted to explore her baser desires and discover her sexuality more fully. That included watching—being a voyeur. The thought of it always turned her on. Now she knew the real thing did, too.

"Answer me."

"Yes." The word flowed out of her, evaporating in the hot air.

"Fuck." Logan bit out the word, his body shuddering against his hand. Cum decorated the pane of glass as he orgasmed.

Not once did his eyes leave hers as he wrung the

last drop of pleasure from his body. Logan's mouth was open, panting.

A shiver ran through her body, and she licked her lips.

"Get out."

She blinked rapidly, trying to understand what had just happened, and retreated a step. "Logan—"

"Get out, Ava." He turned his back to her and started shampooing his hair.

No point in arguing. She was too keyed up to hold a coherent conversation, anyway. One night without doing her skincare routine wouldn't kill her.

She slipped out of the washroom and retreated to her guest suite.

She couldn't believe that happened.

Did she just watch Logan masturbate to her? And more importantly, why was it so gratifying? If she was into anyone, that person was Roman. But the strange, magnetic pull between her and Logan plagued her mind.

She needed to figure out what she was doing with these two men. And do it quickly.

Chapter Seven

AVA

Two days had passed since the shower incident with Logan. Neither of them spoke about it, and she didn't tell Roman since things were already so comfortable with him.

Logan pleasured himself to her *one* time. Once. There was no way he was going to do it again. Even if she wanted him to. Even if the idea of it made her insides melt, and her pulse skyrocket. He was too closed off. She couldn't have two men anyway, and Roman captured her attention from the second she saw him in his pub.

She'd spent Thursday and Friday morning with Roman, eating breakfast in the dining nook before he went to work at his pub. In his absence, she and Logan worked on the B&B. He took one guest bathroom, and she took the other. They'd both finished their respective tasks by Friday afternoon. She'd tiled the shower, installed the vanity, and put in the backsplash—finishing before Logan, which gave her time to do the vanity in her guest bathroom, too. If Logan was impressed with her abilities, he didn't let on. But he wasn't scowling near as much as usual, so she counted that a win.

Roman came home early Friday evening, wanting to show her the hiking paths in the woods behind the B&B. They trekked all the way to Kawawaymog Lake. The stars glittered off the glassy reflection of the water. The lack of excessive city lighting allowed them to shine uninhibited. The entire hike was a ninety-minute round trip, but time passed easily when she was with him. When Roman was around, a contentment spread through her mind and soul.

He often initiated physical contact—brushing her hair out of her face, placing his palm on the small of her back, rubbing her shoulders at the end of the evening. But nothing like that first kiss they shared. The kiss that set every nerve ending on high alert.

She wished he would take it further. Invite her to his room, grasp her neck, and kiss her again. Do something more, for goodness' sake. But it was too soon. His interest in her was obvious, but she hadn't been around long. And she was leaving in five days.

Still, she found she was happier in Little Greenfield with these two men—even Logan—than she had been at home for a long while. The realization was sobering. She did *not* want to return to her life with Sebastian. Roman had shown her more respect, more decency, and more understanding than her ex had in…almost their entire relationship. And she wasn't sure she could count the love bombing at the beginning as decent behaviour. Shithead Sebastian had tainted her life, and she clenched her teeth when she thought of him.

"My time here has been good so far. Getting away was a good decision," she said, sitting at the breakfast counter with Roman, waiting for Logan to finish cooking. The weekend meant they were all together. "I'm glad I had enough time banked at work that I could leave for ten days."

Roman nodded and leaned forward, scooting his stool closer to hers. Logan stood off to the side, making breakfast, clearly listening, but trying to appear like he wasn't.

"I wish I'd given Sebastian a bigger piece of my mind. Or keyed his car. Or hurt him a fraction of how much he hurt me. That's petty though, right?"

Roman shook his head. "The feeling is completely valid. Who wouldn't want to get back at an asshole like that?"

"He has this ratty baseball cap that he wears all the time. I always hated it, but it's his favourite thing in the world. I wish I would have thrown it in the trash after I dumped him. Ripped it right off his stupid head," she grumbled, trying to keep the anger from bubbling over again.

She was making headway here. Little Greenfield was opening her eyes. She'd even started compiling a list to sort her thoughts. A pros and cons list for what she wanted in a relationship. One that would allow her to be her confident, outgoing, sociable self. So, she didn't want her anger clouding her judgement.

"What did you do when you dumped him?" Roman asked, eyes intently locked on hers.

She sighed. "Nothing extraordinary. I told him he hurt me, asked how he could do that to the woman he supposedly loved, then said we were done. I talk a big game, but my follow through doesn't quite match up," she said with a shrug.

"And he just let you leave?"

"I mean, when I confronted him about the message, it was a huge fight. But when he started the…name calling, I walked out the door. I'd heard it enough the day before when I tried to ask for what I wanted in the bedroom. I didn't need to hear it again while I was dumping him."

"Name calling? What is he, twelve years old?" Logan huffed from the stove, loading three plates with back bacon, frittata, and roasted veggies. "What did he call you?"

She rolled her eyes. "A slut, a nympho, a common whore. I'm sure you can see the pattern."

Logan slammed down the cast-iron pan on the

stovetop. He chucked the tea towel on the counter, stormed past her and Roman, and disappeared through the hidden door into the back of the house.

She was dumbfounded.

What did she do to make him *that* mad?

Why was he always so frosty?

After all, he was the one who asked.

"Ignore him," Roman said, covering her hand with his. "He gets like that sometimes."

"How do you live with him?" She shook her head. "He always seems ticked off about something."

He shrugged. "He's my best friend. And there's a big difference between Logan being ticked off *at* you and being ticked off *for* you."

"And which one is he now?"

Roman stroked his fingers over hers. "I'm not quite sure."

She looked away and cleared her throat. "Since Logan's gone, do you mind if I play Sebastian's message for you? I feel you deserve to have the full context of the situation."

"Do you want to? Because I don't need to hear it. It won't change what I think of you."

"And what do you think of me?"

"I think you know," he said, eyes filled with longing.

Her choice. This time, she decided if someone heard it or not. And while the possibility of Roman being disgusted by her gave her an empty feeling in the pit of her stomach, part of her needed him to know. If she was going to figure out what she wanted, then Roman needed to know everything. This would be the quickest way to gauge whether what he thought of her was genuine or surface level.

Her mouth felt dry and her finger twitched when she clicked open the message from Sebastian on her phone. She hit play and his smarmy voice filled the kitchen.

Roman got a fire going in the outdoor pit. After throwing on a sweater, she joined him on one of the outdoor loveseats under a light blanket. A warm breeze blowing through the clear night air, and sitting outside by the fire with Roman seemed like the best evening she could ask for right now. How they hadn't had one until now was beyond her.

Letting Roman listen to Sebastian's cruel message had been the right choice. He stayed quiet until the very end, when he let out a string of vulgar curses she would be embarrassed to repeat. Then his arms wrapped around her in the bear hug of the century. When he finally pulled back from their embrace, he took her face in both his thick, calloused hands and told her she wasn't a deviant. Nothing was wrong with her. That any man would be privileged to give her what she wanted. The glimmer in his eye when he uttered those words told her he wanted to be that man.

They'd spent the rest of Saturday together. His employees had the day covered at the pub. He didn't need to go in, so he could spend time with her. The afternoon flew by as she used her marketing expertise to help him brainstorm potential for the B&B. What did they offer that was unique? What was the main draw to Little Greenfield? Who were their competitors?

She wasn't sure how things clicked so quickly with Roman, but she wasn't going to over analyze anything right now. Sebastian was old news. She was embracing what she wanted. Right now, that was Roman.

He joined her on the loveseat, snaking his arm around her waist. "Ava," he said, trailing his fingers down her neck, tracing a path to the top of her breasts and down her arms, making her feverish with need. "There are so many things I want to do for you."

She ran her palm across his burgundy Henley, taking pleasure in the feel of his broad chest. Her touch was the only sign that Roman needed. His mouth dipped to meet her own, and his tongue licked between her lips. She opened, sighing into his mouth, relieved to finally feel it on hers again.

He pawed at her underneath the blanket, finding her hips and effortlessly lifting her to straddle him in the firelight. He was hard beneath her, and she pressed into him, getting off on the friction.

"I've been desperate to feel you again, love." His large hand slipped underneath her sweater to shamelessly squeeze her breast. "Is this okay?"

"More than okay." His consideration spurred her on and she found herself riding Roman's cock through his jeans, desperately aching to feel him any way she could.

"Fuck, Ava. Keep going like that and I'm going to come in my pants."

"I'd rather you come on me," she whispered in his ear. She was playing a dangerous game.

Roman made quick work of undoing her jean short's button and zipper to loosen the waistband. He shoved his hand down the back of her thong, massaging her ass, working his way further down to the place she really wanted him to touch.

"Take me out," he groaned, licking at her neck as a finger circled her entrance, never once losing his focus on her pleasure.

Her hands flew to his belt, and she wrestled open his chinos, her mouth watering at the idea of seeing his cock. At holding it in her hands. "I need to feel you, Roman, I need to—"

Logan's motorcycle barrelled down the winding road toward the bed and breakfast. He'd been gone all day.

"Fuck," Roman bit out, removing his hand from her shorts.

She whimpered at the loss of his touch.

"Later, love. We'll pick this up later, I promise."

He gently helped Ava off his lap and made himself decent while she did the same. Couldn't a girl catch a break?

Parking next to Roman's truck, Logan swung his leg over the seat and removed his helmet. A maneuver that would've been sexy if it weren't coming from the frosty ice man of Little Greenfield. He grabbed a bag from the compartment behind the seat and stalked to where she and Roman were sitting.

After storming out of the kitchen that morning, he took off without a word to either of them. He didn't respond to any of Roman's text messages, either. So they let it be.

Roman gave her one last lingering kiss, then rose and stepped in front of Logan, stopping him in his tracks with a palm to his chest. Whispering something to him that she couldn't make out, Logan took a deep breath and slowed his roll.

She hadn't been staying with them long, only five days, but she already knew that Roman could cool Logan down with a few well-placed words when needed. The same way he could reassure and comfort her when she needed it most.

After a beat, Roman let Logan pass by him to

stand in front of her. Digging in his bag, he pulled out a dingy-looking thing and tossed it on her lap.

"Hey!" she yelped, affronted. "What is this supposed to—?"

The words caught in her throat.

A hat.

The hat.

Sebastian's ugly, stupid, ratty old hat that he loved more than anything in the world.

How the heck did Logan get this?

"Where did you—? How did you—?" She stared dumbstruck at the hat on her lap. She was truly at a loss for words.

When she peered up from her seat on the sofa, she found Logan staring at her with an odd expression. Was it her imagination, or did his normally hard eyes seem a tad softer? Before she could say or do anything, he stalked away toward the cabin.

Was this where he was today?

He drove five hours to the city and five hours back to get Sebastian's ugly-ass hat for her?

How did he know where he lived?

How did he get the freaking hat?

"Did he see you?" she called after Logan, who was halfway to the B&B's front door. "Did you talk to him?" Her heart picked up speed and sweat gathered on her palms.

"No," Logan replied. "He has no idea."

She breathed a sigh of relief. The last thing she wanted was Sebastian's ire directed at Logan.

"I keyed his car, too." Logan's normally abrasive tone held a hint of amusement. The door slammed shut behind him.

Beside her, a deep chuckle poured from Roman's throat. He flopped down on the loveseat beside her, a mile-wide grin plastered on his face.

"I think he likes you," he teased.

"I think…" She shook her head. "I don't know what to think."

Logan had been so hot and cold to her since the minute she arrived. One moment he was stripping in front of her in the bathroom, the next he was icing her out and pretending she didn't exist. So exhausting.

But—if she was honest—also kind of exhilarating.

"What are you going to do with the hat?" Roman asked, slipping his hand onto her knee. His thumb brushed back and forth. "Hold it for ransom?" Another cheeky smile graced his lips.

"No way. Sebastian is never getting this back."

She walked to the fire pit and held the hat above the roaring flames. A wicked grin filled her face.

"I'm going to burn it." Her gaze shifted to the cabin. "Then I'm going to get answers."

Chapter Eight

AVA

She closed her eyes and took an expansive breath before entering the cabin. Logan was in the kitchen, doing dishes from earlier in the day. It struck her as odd, seeing him do something so domestic. He was always busy working on the bed and breakfast or taking one of the work trucks out to get supplies. Seeing him elbows deep in soapy dishwater was an entirely new experience. It didn't suit him, but it softened a few of his rough edges.

Her hands trembled when she walked toward him. Forearms covered in bubbles, Logan was still formidable. Where to start?

"Logan…thank you for getting the hat for me. Can we talk about it?" It took a great deal of concentration not to let her voice crack. In addition to being nervous, she was overcome with gratitude at what he'd done for her.

Without looking at her, he continued washing dishes and setting them on the drying rack. "There's nothing to talk about."

She rubbed her forehead. A coy approach wouldn't work with him. She had to be direct. "I think there is. You stormed out of here this morning, and were gone the whole day. No one knew where you went. You didn't answer your phone. Then you come strutting back tonight with Sebastian's hat in your bag."

"And?"

"And that's bizarre! How did you even find out where he lives? I never told you his last name."

"It's really not that hard, Ava. Nowadays, everyone puts everything on the internet."

"So you found him online? No big deal?"

"No big deal."

Not once in the entire conversation had Logan glanced up at her. He finished washing, grabbed a dish towel, and began to dry each piece of tableware. It's like this meant nothing to him. But why would he do it, then? If he didn't care? Obviously, this was a major gesture. He was refusing to acknowledge it, and that stirred the confusion inside her chest.

She blew out her cheeks. "It *is* a big deal, Logan. To me."

Nothing.

She wandered into the foyer, considering going outside to Roman. To the warm fire. To where she felt comfortable. She shook her head, steeled her shoulders, and marched back to the kitchen.

"Logan—look at me."

He slammed down the mixing bowl he was drying, threw the dish towel over his shoulder, and finally met her gaze.

"Tell me why you did this." Her body grew hot under his full attention.

His eyes narrowed, and he clenched and unclenched his jaw. He grasped the edge of the counter that stood between them and offered one word. "Because."

"That is not an answer, Logan!" God, did he always have to be so infuriating? Do some grand gesture, then pretend like it's not significant? "Talk to me."

There was no mistaking the tension in his neck, shoulders, and arms. The veins were practically bulging out of his skin. If she wasn't so annoyed with him, those arms might've aroused her.

"Because Sebastian is a fuckface bastard who needed to be taught a lesson. Who is he to tell dozens of people you're a sexual deviant?" His hands squeezed into fists before plunging through his hair. "There's nothing wrong with the things you like. Nothing."

"How would you know that?"

He crossed his arms and stared at her. Long and hard. The intensity of his regard almost made her break their gaze, but she held her ground. This was the most he'd ever spoken to her, and he'd finally said something of consequence.

He'd listened to what she said this morning.

He'd punished Sebastian for her.

He'd stood up for her.

This is what Roman meant when he said Logan could be pissed off *for* you.

She went around the counter and placed her palm on his cheek. He didn't pull away. There was no way he was going to answer her question. His stony demeanor said as much. He really was beautiful. More so when he was angry on her behalf.

She withdrew one of his crossed arms and placed his palm on her breastbone, holding his arm close. The tension slowly melted out of his shoulders, and his eyes flickered shut. He leaned forward and placed his head against hers.

"No one gets to call you a slut," he whispered into her hair. His hand crept from her breastbone to wrap lightly around her throat. "Not unless you want them to."

A shiver traveled down her neck and spine to land in her pussy. The gesture was incredibly intimate, and she didn't know what to make of it.

Logan stepped closer to her, and she breathed him

in. He smelled faintly of leather. The tenderness of the moment played games with her head.

She opened her mouth to say something, anything, but before she could say a word, Logan released her and strode to the door that led to the back of the cabin.

"Good night, Ava."

ROMAN

Ava never came back outside. Whatever Logan did or said to her had definitely made an impact. Roman had extinguished the fire and expected to find her in the kitchen or living area. When he'd climbed the stairs to the guest rooms, her door was closed. He didn't want to intrude.

Instead, he'd been standing in his doorway for the past forty-five minutes, waiting for her to use the bathroom before going to bed. He needed to see her before she turned in for the night. Over the past few days, the sexual tension had been building between them and finally poured out during their bonfire. Now, if he didn't do something about it, he was going to erupt.

Finally, the hidden panel opened. He couldn't keep the smile off his face as he watched her silently tip-toe into the hallway, so she wouldn't disturb Logan or him. She'd changed out of the clothes she wore by the fire. Now in a skimpy pink tank top and those goddamn booty shorts she seemed to like to sleep in, he could hardly contain himself.

When she noticed him in the threshold to his bedroom, she jumped and her hand flew to her chest. "You scared the hell out of me, Roman." She blew out a calming breath. "What are you doing?"

Roman strode toward her, his heartbeat pounding in his ears. Now or never. "I was waiting for you."

"Is something wrong?" she asked, her eyes widening with concern as he stopped in front of her. "Did I mess up the backsplash install? Because the grout was being particularly difficult, but I swear I—"

"Ava, stop." He kept his voice soft, but firm. "You haven't done anything wrong." He took a step closer to her. "You've been nothing but wonderful."

"Oh." Her gaze explored his face. "What is it then? Is there something else you need me to take care of?"

He pushed her against the wall. A sharp intake of breath left her lips. Trailing a finger across her collar bone, he looked her in the eyes, never breaking their gaze. "Let me take care of you, love. I'm dying to show you how good we can be."

"We barely know each other, Roman. Should we be doing this?" Ava asked softly, but she didn't draw back.

He saw the rise and fall of her chest quicken. She

definitely wanted this, but she needed to get out of her head. He needed to show her she had nothing to be ashamed of. Nothing to be embarrassed about. Ava was allowed to want him. It didn't matter that it had been less than a week.

He felt the heat between them every time they were together. Every time he touched her arm or brushed aside her hair. Every time she playfully pushed his shoulder. When she was grinding on his cock and they were both fully clothed.

"That doesn't matter." He placed one arm on the wall beside her. "We know enough to recognize we're attracted to each other. We know we work well together. And you know I'll take care of you."

Leaning down, he ran his lips across the side of her neck. She tipped her head ever-so-slightly to the side to give him better access.

"Tell me you want this too," he breathed in her ear.

"I want this."

With those words, he bit down on the crook of her neck, and she gave a sharp cry. He wrapped his arms around her waist, holding her tight as he licked into her mouth.

Ava's lips parted for him hungrily. Her breathing became ragged against his mouth, and her hands flew into his hair. His tongue danced with hers, and the sweet taste of her was enough to make him weak in the knees. She tugged at his shirt, urging him to deepen the kiss.

Hoisting her legs around his waist, he carried her toward his bedroom. Her ass was round and firm in his hands. He couldn't wait to see it bare.

"Tell me what you want, Ava," he whispered against her mouth in between kisses. "I'll do anything you want. Try anything. Give you anything."

She was quiet. In her head again.

"There's no shame here. It's just me and you. Let me help you explore."

Ava nodded. Slowly at first, then with more confidence. "Okay."

"There's nothing I wouldn't do to you, love. Or let you do to me." He walked her over to his bed and laid her down gently. "To be honest, I've been dying to get you in my bed from the moment I saw you sitting at my bar."

Staring at him, she seemed shocked. "Really?"

"Are you kidding? Your full lips. Those striking blue eyes. That firm fucking ass. You're a total smokeshow." He nipped at her bottom lip.

She blushed at his words. "And you weren't… um…you weren't freaked out by all the things on the voice message?"

She looked so earnest he couldn't help but let out a laugh.

"God, Ava." He nuzzled her neck, inhaling her

heady lavender scent. "No part of me was freaked out."

Her hands pushed at his chest, and he lifted himself to meet her gaze.

"No part at all?"

Roman's hand moved to his belt, unbuckling it and pulling it out of the belt loops slowly. He grasped her hands and placed them above her head. "None." He laced the belt around her wrists like the voice message had mentioned. "It made me want to do every one of those things to you."

He secured the belt tight, binding her wrists.

"Every. Single. One."

Ava's mouth fell open. This was going to be even more enjoyable than he thought. It would be him who got to give Ava everything she wanted. And he meant it when he said he would do anything. Five days with her in his B&B and he was completely taken by her.

He secured the belt to a slat in his headboard. Tight enough to keep her arms above her head, but not so tight that she'd be uncomfortable.

"But before we get started," he said, lifting her tank top slowly and deliberately. "I'm going to do something for me." He traced his fingers over her full breasts and pink nipples.

Tugging off her shorts, he dipped his head to taste her through the lacy fabric of her thong. A loud groan left his lips. A sharp gasp came from hers.

He sucked her through the fabric until he couldn't

take the separation anymore. Roughly pushing her soaked underwear to the side, his tongue found her clit.

Ava's hips bucked against his face, and he used one forearm across her pelvis to keep her steady. He licked and sucked at her sensitive spot, responding when her moans grew louder, learning what worked for her and what didn't.

The taste of her on his tongue was everything he fantasized it would be. Her soft skin under his rough hands drove him wild. Touching it wasn't enough. He groped her hips and thighs, kneading them as he reveled in how her cunt felt pressed against his mouth.

Ava responded so well to him. He peered up at her while her clit was on his tongue, taking in the sight of her head thrown back against the sheets, her hands straining against his belt. She was a force.

"You look like fucking heaven."

"More." The cry flew from her lips. The bed slat creaked with the strain of Ava pulling against the belt.

Roman licked her like a starving man, shoving two fingers deep into her pussy to help drive her to the edge. He found a motion that made her breathing pick up, and he kept it steady. Her walls pulsed around his fingers. Moans became needy and frantic. He kept the pace, her body tensing underneath his forearm, and he knew she was going to come.

Ava let out a scream and warmth flooded Roman's face. He ate her through her orgasm, lapping at any bit of arousal he could get his tongue on. His fingers were dripping, and his cock was aching to be inside her. Nothing turned him on like making a woman squirt all over his face. Her pleasure was like a drug to him. He wanted more.

"That's so fucking hot, Ava. I wanna make you do that again."

Licking his way up her slack body, he put his mouth on every part of her. Her hip bones, her belly, the dip between her breasts. He took one nipple in his mouth and sucked hard. A long groan escaped Ava's lips, and he bit down playfully, causing her to emerge from her post-orgasm high.

"Roman…"

"Yes, love?" he murmured against her skin, sucking her other nipple into his mouth and lavishing it with the same attention. The hard bud against his tongue was intoxicating. "Tell me what you want."

"Anything?"

His hands lifted to the belt that kept her arms above her head. Undoing the strap from the bed slat and her wrists, he said, "Anything. Let's explore."

"Can we…role-play? That I don't want it?" A rosy blush flooded her cheeks.

"Do you feel safe enough with me for that?"

Ava nodded.

"Of course we can." He nuzzled the crook of her neck. "Is that what you want for our first time together?"

"As long as you're okay with it. I've wanted to try it for a long time, but…" She looked away from him.

He gently took her chin and directed her gaze to his own. "I'm down for anything with you, love. But we need a safe word you can use to stop the situation if it gets too intense. Or for any other reason."

She thought for a second. "Peanut butter."

"Peanut butter? Really?"

"Why not?" She ran her fingers through his hair. "Seems appropriate."

"Fine by me, love. Do you have a scene in mind?"

"No," she admitted. "I've done nothing like this before. Can you take the lead?"

"With pleasure." He kissed down her arm, ending with a press of his lips to her wrist, then crawled out of bed. "Remember—say peanut butter and we stop immediately."

Chapter Nine

AVA

Her entire being vibrated with anticipation as she stripped off her thong and tank top. Lying naked in Roman's bed, she waited for him to reappear in the doorway. He left moments ago, and the excitement of what would happen next had her knees shaking.

Sebastian had been the most upset about this request. He didn't want to pretend with her. In fact, he told her she was messed up in the head for wanting something like this. No one actually role-played these things, he told her. And wanting a man to force himself on her while she struggled against him? That was out of the question, even consensually. He told her she was sick and needed therapy.

Yet, here was Roman. Ready at the drop of a hat to accommodate her desires and allow her to try this out. To see if she really wanted it. Judging by how wet she was just waiting for him, it was safe to say she did. She wanted it bad.

"I've been watching you, blondie."

Roman appeared in the doorway, standing in nothing but his pants. His deep voice was more gravelly than usual. It had a menacing tone to it. Shivers swept across her body.

"How'd you get in here?" she asked.

"The front door was open. You practically invited me in," he said, stepping closer to the bed.

"It wasn't," she said, gripping the bed sheets tight to her body to cover her nakedness.

"Baby, you've been lounging naked in that bed all evening, your tits and ass on display for anyone to see out those windows." He flicked his gaze to the floor-to-ceiling windows that faced the forest behind the property. "You looked like you wanted a real man to come in here and give you a good fuck. Isn't that right, baby? Or were you teasing me?"

"I didn't realize anyone was watching me. I promise I wasn't teasing you. Please leave." Her voice was thick and husky, betraying what she actually wanted.

Roman crossed the rest of the way to the bed and started undoing his chinos. "That's not what you really want."

He ripped the sheets away from her body, and she covered herself with her hands. Climbing on top of her, he pushed her down against the bed and covered her mouth with his hand.

"Get off me!" she tried to yell, but her words were muffled against his palm. Her hands hit his shoulders, and she tried to push him away, push him off her, but his large frame made it impossible. Her pulse skyrocketed and her pussy fluttered.

"Fight it if you want, baby, but you teased my cock all day, roaming around the house in those skimpy shorts. Putting yourself on show. I'm taking what's mine," he snarled in her ear.

If she had panties on, they would've melted. He knew exactly what to say and do. It took everything in her not to moan against his hand.

"I think you want it just as much as me." His free hand roughly cupped her pussy and two fingers slipped forcefully between her folds, rubbing her. "You're soaked," he sneered.

His fingers plunged inside her, rough and raw and rude. He pumped them in and up against her most sensitive spot. She bucked against him, losing her will to fight, wanting to give in to the ecstasy. The sudden loss of his fingers had her calling out.

"Don't worry, baby. I'm going to have you screaming by the time I'm done with you." He yanked down his waistband until his cock sprung free. "See what you do to me? It's only fair that you finish what you started, blondie. Like it or not."

She couldn't believe her eyes. Roman's dick was long and broad, matching the rest of him. Along his shaft, halfway between the head and base of his cock, he had a silver piercing. Her mouth watered. She wanted to lick it.

Grabbing her waist, he flipped her over so fast her brain had to play catch up. Roman's hand on the back of her neck held her down on the bed.

She pushed against him, trying to force him away from her, playing into the scene they'd built together. "I don't want this. I don't want you."

"Shut your filthy mouth," he snarled in her ear. Heat radiated off him. "No one else is here. No one can hear you scream."

Foil ripped and a condom wrapper landed on the bed next to her face. His cock notched at her entrance and he groaned. "I'm going to fuck you hard. I don't care how much it hurts or how much you beg me not to. This cunt is mine for the night, blondie."

Roman shoved into her from behind, and she let loose. A scream of pleasure erupted from her. The entire scene was so wrong, so filthy, so naughty—she loved it. His piercing rubbed at her in a way that had her squirming back against him, greedy for more.

Roman landed a loud smack on the side of her backside. "Tell me you want it, baby. Otherwise, I'll make this ass of yours bright red."

"I want it."

"Make me believe it." Another sharp slap landed on her ass.

"I want you to fuck me. Do whatever you want to me." She moaned into Roman's sheets, holding on to them for purchase. He was satisfying all her dirty fantasies.

His frame pressed down on her, shoving her flat into the bed. He bucked inside her, thrusting like a man possessed. Every muscle, every inch of his skin was flush against her. He roughly cupped her jaw and wrenched her head toward him. "Tell me you're mine."

"I'm yours." And she truly wanted to be.

He claimed her mouth with a harsh kiss, biting at her lower lip, invading her mouth with his tongue. One hand slid between the mattress and her body, finding her clit with ease. He stroked her, and she jerked against him.

"Scream for me, baby. Be a good girl and let me know how perfect my dick feels in your soaking wet pussy."

Ava couldn't contain herself any longer. She cried out his name into the bedsheets, jolting against his body, which pinned her to the bed. He didn't let up. Roman fucked her through her orgasm, continuing to play with her clit, and she came so hard her vision temporarily went black.

Roman stuttered out his release, rocking against

her. Then his arms were around her waist, lifting her onto his lap. He stroked her hair and ran his palm down her arm, cradling her to him.

"Are you okay, Ava?"

She hummed dreamily. "I'm better than okay. That was amazing. I loved it."

His laugh rumbled against her cheek, and he held her for a long moment. "I'm going to get a glass of water for you and a cloth to clean you with." The condom landed in his garbage can with a plop, and he began to stand.

"No, don't go." She pounced on him, knocking him flat on the bed. "Stay with me."

"I'll come right back. Aftercare is important, Ava. Especially in scenes like this."

She nodded against him, liking how his chest hair rubbed against her face. "But I want a few more minutes like this."

"Of course." He wrapped his tattooed arms around her once more and held her tight against his torso.

Ava was flushed and sweaty, as was Roman, but it didn't stop her from climbing on top of him and holding him tightly. She traced the flowers inked on his neck with her fingertips. "Thank you."

"Trust me, the pleasure's all mine."

She peppered kisses across his chest, taking time to kiss each one of his nipples, and worked her way to his Adam's apple. "I can't thank you enough. I've always wanted to do that."

"Like I said…anything, Ava. I'll do anything for you."

"Let me show you how much I appreciate you."

A low chuckle broke free from his chest. "I think you just did."

She sat up, straddling him, and shimmied herself backward until she was in line with his pelvis. A quick grind of her hips revealed he was still semi-hard. She arched her back and put her hands on his upper thighs.

"Ava, what are you doing?"

"Showing you my appreciation."

She skimmed a finger down her neck toward her breasts. When she pinched her nipple and gave it a twist, Roman groaned underneath her and bucked his hips. Her mouth dropped open at the pleasure of his cock between her slit. Moving her body forward and backward, she glided her pussy over his dick, sliding it bare against her clit. She was wracked with shivers from head to toe.

"Ava," Roman warned. "You're playing a dangerous game."

Not answering him, she closed her eyes to focus on the sensation. He was so smooth against her without a condom. His flesh on hers, without a barrier, was heavenly. Her pace picked up, spreading her wetness everywhere on his cock. The piercing along his shaft rubbed her clit just right, and she moaned each time she brushed it, unable to help herself.

Roman gave in and grabbed her hips, helping her slide over his length. He was fully hard again, and she wanted to bring him another release.

"Fuck, Ava. Fuck, fuck, fuck. I'm not even inside you and it feels fucking incredible." His head dropped against the sheets in a low groan of ecstasy as he moved her along his shaft.

Ava opened her eyes and saw Logan standing in the doorway, leaning against the frame. Watching them. Watching her. Roman must've forgotten to close the door when he entered for their scene. How much had Logan heard? How long had he been standing there?

She didn't stop. Roman's bare cock felt too good against her swollen pussy to put an end to this prematurely. And seeing Logan's gaze roam from her lips, to her tits, down to her bare cunt, and up again was turning her on twice as much.

They made eye contact, and she didn't back down. She held his gaze in a challenge. While gliding on Roman's dick, she traced her fingers across her breasts and down her stomach until she reached her pussy. Slipping one finger between her folds, she found her clit and began to play. She tilted her head, as if to say to Logan, *what are you going to do about it?*

His hand took hold of the zipper on his jeans, dragging it down lazily. Reaching inside his underwear, he pulled out his cock.

It seemed heavy in his grasp. With one long lick to his palm, he gripped himself tight and began to stroke. All while never breaking eye contact with her. She trembled under his watchful eye.

"I need to be inside you again, Ava. Please say you're on the pill. Please tell me I can fuck you bare."

The idea of Roman inside her with nothing between them while Logan watched and fucked his own hand was everything her wildest dreams were made of. She leaned forward and kissed Roman. "Yes." She bit his lower lip, making him twitch underneath her. "And yes."

She took hold of his dick and angled it up, spreading her legs wide and sinking down on it. The sound from his lips was pure filth. They were joined with nothing between them, and Logan watched the whole thing. He saw her slide down Roman's bare cock, and he stroked himself even faster.

"You feel so fucking good, love. So wet and ready for me."

They moved in unison. She rode him slowly at first, his hands guiding her movements while he thrust into her from underneath.

Logan reached into his back pocket with his unoccupied hand and withdrew something. Bright pink fabric. He wrapped it around his erection and continued stroking.

That's when it clicked.

Her thong.

Her missing thong.

Logan had taken it, and now he was using it to get off while he watched her fuck his best friend.

Her pussy fluttered and squeezed Roman's firm dick. She was tempted to throw her head back and let the orgasm take her, but she kept her eyes locked on Logan. She wanted him to get off at the same time they did. Ava dropped her hands to Roman's shoulders, using them to help her rock her hips into a frenzy.

"I need you to come with me." She said it to Roman, but meant it for Logan, too. For both of them.

Roman faltered beneath her, his orgasm rocking through his body. Logan jolted, and she watched him release into her underwear, covering it with his cum. She slapped her clit hard, and bit back a cry as she came alongside both of them.

Ava collapsed on Roman. Their chests were slick with sweat, heaving together while arousal pooled between their legs. She kissed his neck, his jaw, his ear, then rested her head on his. Completely relaxed, almost weightless, she hummed in appreciation.

This was what sex was supposed to be.

Raw. Carnal. Consuming.

Roman removed himself from her, and she mourned the loss. He extricated himself from their embrace with care and placed a pillow under Ava's head.

"How are you feeling?" The touch of his fingers against her cheek was sweet and gentle.

"Blissed out." Her head tipped back, and she stared at the ceiling. The tension drained out of her body. She angled her head toward the doorway. Logan was gone.

Roman grinned. "Can I get us some water and a towel now?"

"Yes, please. And a snack?"

"Sure. Don't go anywhere." He gave her a quick peck on the nose, threw on a pair of sweats, and left the room.

Ava had no idea where this would lead, but she felt liberated. Plainly stating what she wanted and taking it. Opening herself to new experiences and relationships. Discovering the things she wanted and admired in a partner. She made a mental note to add *begging, being watched,* and *aftercare* to her relationship pros list.

She liked the Ava she was becoming in Little Greenfield. In this place, she was so much more authentic to herself. What started out as wanting to get away from Sebastian's humiliating actions was turning into something much more.

Roman accepted her as she was. As much as she

didn't come here searching for someone new, she couldn't help but admit he definitely felt like someone she could see herself with.

So what was she doing with Logan?

Chapter Ten

ROMAN

Was that the most mind-blowing sex he'd ever had? Abso-fucking-lutely. Ava was a spitfire. He couldn't make sense of her last boyfriend telling her off. What a spineless jag.

She'd trusted Roman enough to let him pin her down and fuck her like a stranger. She let him inside her without a condom. For all that is holy, he came inside her. Five days with her, and he was smitten. Completely and utterly smitten.

It wasn't only the sex, although that was a tremendous bonus. He was drawn to everything about her. The strength it took to finally leave her ex. The willingness to jump in and help finish the B&B without being asked. How she was keen to do mundane things like picking out furniture for the balcony. The way her laugh filled a room. How her hair bounced when she walked. He lost track of time when he was with her.

But something was going on with Logan that needed to be dealt with. Did he think Roman hadn't heard him in the doorway, touching himself to the sight of Ava bouncing on his cock?

The one reason he hadn't got up and laid him out was knowing Ava had exhibitionist fantasies. But how did Logan know?

It wasn't like him to invade such an intimate time. Unless he was invited, of course. They'd shared before, when they were in their twenties, but only a handful of times, and only at the request of the woman. And those were one-night stands.

Ava was different. She wasn't a one-time fling. Logan needed to understand this wasn't fucking for the sake of fucking. He had genuine feelings for her. Ava was his, and he was hers.

He stalked down the hall toward Logan's room. They were going to have this out right here, right now—or he was going to combust.

He didn't bother knocking. Instead, he threw the door open. But Logan wasn't there. He stomped into the main house and found him in the living area, stretched out on a couch under the light of a single lamp.

"What the hell do you think you're doing?" He ground his teeth to keep from yelling as he stormed toward his best friend while waiting for his reply. Logan wasn't his rival. He had to remember that.

Logan scrolled through his phone. He didn't even do Roman the courtesy of looking up.

"Ava's waiting, so answer me, Logan. You've been acting like a royal dick since she got here. And now you think you can watch her and me like we're some sort of peep show?"

Logan's head snapped toward him. He sat forward and tossed his phone on the coffee table, shoving the hair out of his eyes. "I don't know what I'm doing, okay, Banks? I have no fucking clue."

The admission stopped Roman in his tracks.

Logan had a hard time being vulnerable. Admitting when he was lost or confused.

Roman sat on the couch by his best friend. "Talk to me. What's going on?"

Logan crossed his arms. "I'm pissed off."

"Yeah, I gathered as much. Why?"

A pinched expression twisted his face. "Because you met her first."

Roman's mouth fell open. "You like her?"

"I don't know!" He scrubbed his hand over his jaw. "There's something between us. I feel it every time I'm near her."

"What do you want me to say?"

Logan grimaced and shook his head.

A heavy silence settled between them. Roman took a beat to study Logan. His shoulders were slumped, his eyes had bags underneath, and his usual bravado was gone.

With a heavy sigh, he asked the question weighing on his mind. "Did Ava play you the message from Sebastian?"

"Not exactly."

"Explain."

"I opened her phone while you were both out the other day and sent it to myself."

Roman stilled, blinking his eyes slowly. "You what?"

"I had to find out what the big deal was. What could be so bad she had to run away? So I sent that message to myself."

"And you listened to it?"

Logan didn't reply.

"Logan?" Roman stared him down.

"Yes, I listened to it. Not all of it, but a decent portion."

"Did you tell Ava?"

He scowled. "No fucking way."

"No fucking way is right. She's gonna be pissed, man. But you have to tell her."

Logan's shoulders slumped. "I know. I gotta find the right time."

Roman nodded. A sharp pain stabbed in his chest because he knew what else needed to happen. "You need to figure out what this thing between you two is."

He let out a loud sigh. "You mean it?"

"Listen, I'm falling for her. For me, this isn't a game. And if there is something between you two that needs to get worked out, or resolved, or—fuck, explored—then so be it. It's up to her what she wants, not me."

Logan brightened a fraction. "And you think she'd be okay with this?"

"You listened to the first part of the voice message. You know she's not necessarily looking for a traditional relationship. Maybe this is what she wants. Who am I to deny her that? I simply want to see her happy."

His eyebrows knitted together. "And that's something you could be into?"

"Could you?"

"We've shared before."

"Not seriously. Not an actual relationship." Roman frowned and popped his knuckles absentmindedly.

He'd never been in a poly relationship before. But then again, he'd never met a woman that made him consider the option. He said he'd do anything for Ava. And if she wanted to be with more than one man, he couldn't think of a better one than Logan. Sure, he was a dickhole sometimes, but he was hard-working, honest, and cared deeply about the people who mattered to him.

Sharing her though…that's something he'd have to get used to.

Logan sank against the couch. "We're not even sure she feels the same way."

"Well, you must have an idea, otherwise you wouldn't have put on your little show in my doorway tonight."

He rubbed his hands on his jeans. "There may have been a moment or two between us this week."

Roman closed his eyes and nodded, processing the new information. "Tomorrow, you're taking Ava somewhere. Improvise an errand or something and ask her to go with you. Talk to her. Get to know her. See what happens and if you can't sort yourself out."

Sitting up, Logan said, "After what I just did, I think I should talk to her now."

"No," Roman said, more forcefully than he'd intended. "We shared had an intense role-play session, and then she let me fuck her raw. This is my night with her, not yours."

Roman strode into the kitchen. He grabbed two bottles of water, a plate of fruit leftover from yesterday's lunch, and a clean washcloth that he warmed with water from the sink.

"Get some sleep, and figure out what you want to do. But if you do go out tomorrow, let her lead. And if she wants to try it on with you, so be it."

"Just so we're clear—try it on with me means…" Logan hesitated.

"Fucking. If she wants to fuck you, then go for it. We'll work out what it means later." With that, Roman left Logan behind, and made his way to his room where Ava was patiently waiting for him.

"I was about to send a search party for you," Ava teased, sitting in the middle of Roman's bed.

God, she was beautiful. Her blonde hair was tangled and fell over her tits. The sheets pooled in her lap, obscuring the rest of her body. His radiant siren, luring him into her trap. One he'd happily dive into.

He handed her the plate of fruit and a bottle of water, then stripped off his sweats. "Sorry, love. Had to talk to Logan for a minute."

She raised her eyebrows, but said nothing. Instead, she shoveled grapes into her mouth, followed by a whole strawberry. Roman didn't push the subject. Logan would talk with her tomorrow, then they would all work something out if necessary. They had to. There was no way he could lose this woman. One day together, five days together—it didn't matter. He knew in his gut she was it for him.

He tugged the sheets out of her lap and began to wipe her inner thighs.

Ava's hand shot out and clasped his wrist. "You don't have to do that."

"I know I don't have to. I want to."

A soft smile graced her face. "You do?"

"Of course I do. I want to take care of you." He resumed gently washing her, spreading her legs and slowly wiping the warm cloth across the parts of her that might need it.

She twirled a blonde curl around her finger as she watched him. "No one's ever offered to take care of me like this."

"What do you say to sleeping here tonight?"

She coughed, clearly caught by surprise. "In your room?" she mumbled around the fruit in her mouth.

God, she was cute.

Hanging the cloth off the top of his nightstand to dry, he opened his water bottle and took a swig. "Yes, in my room."

She beamed. "I think I'd love that."

"Good. I think I'd love that too." Roman joined her on the bed, drawing her close, and settled her between his legs. With her back resting against his chest, he breathed in the lavender scent of her hair.

"Is this what you do with all the girls?"

His face scrunched. "All the girls?"

"Yeah, you know, the girls you bring to your cozy B&B after you've charmed the pants off of them."

He could tell she was fishing. Well, there was nothing for her to catch. "To tell you the truth, love, there haven't been many women in recent years."

Her snort filled the room as she slipped another strawberry into her mouth. "I can't believe that."

Roman slid sideways, and she shifted too, so they looked at each other. "Why can't you believe that?"

"Um…have you seen yourself?"

He had to laugh at that. "I have. But I'm not everyone's cup of tea."

"Well, you're a lot of women's cups of tea. And probably a decent amount of men, too. You're certainly mine."

He plopped a grape in his mouth. "I guess I'm searching for something more serious. You probably don't want to hear that, considering we just met, but there's no point in lying. I'm ready for the next step in my life."

Ava wriggled out of his arms to face him fully, setting the fruit plate aside. She sat between his legs with her knees against her chest. "What's the next step?" Her eyes said she was curious. Not scared or freaked out by his admission.

"Love," he admitted simply. "A long-term relationship. I'm in my mid-thirties. It's time. A relationship like my parents have is what I've wanted for a number of years now."

She placed her palm on his thigh. "What are they like?"

"They're as in love today as they were almost four decades ago when they first met. My dad is a royal goofball, and my mom is more serious. They balance each other out perfectly. It's easy to see why they believe in love at first sight. They click."

She squeezed his leg. "That's beautiful, Roman."

"Yeah, it is. I want that with someone. The effortlessness, the trust, the companionship. Most of all, the devotion and passion they still have after all these years."

She raised an eyebrow at him, making her forehead wrinkle in the most adorable way. "Passion? They must be, what…in their sixties?"

"And going at it like rabbits, I'm afraid."

She grimaced. "Do I want to know how you know that?"

He scrubbed his face with his hands and let his head rest against the headboard. "Let's say I've learned to always call before stopping by."

Her eyes lit up, and she smacked his chest playfully. "You walked in on them?" she squealed.

"I did. On two separate occasions. Now I schedule my visits ahead of time, or let them know I'm on my way over well in advance."

Ava broke out into a fit of hysterics, and he couldn't help but join her. "I would pay handsomely to go back in time and be a fly on that wall."

"Oh no, you wouldn't. Having to see two golden oldies go at it is definitely not worth seeing the expression on my face when I caught them."

"I imagine it was something like this." She pulled a face, squinting her eyes and pursing her lips. A solid effort.

He loved how she felt comfortable enough to goof around with him.

"Actually, it was more like this." He opened his eyes as wide as possible and dropped his jaw in a mock scream of terror, shielding his face with his hands.

Giggles burst out of her again, and he couldn't help thinking he'd love to hear that sound every day for the foreseeable future. He caught hold of her waist and hauled her into his arms, where she belonged.

She settled against him, and he relished the weight against his body, grounding him with her presence. "So…you're looking for a love like theirs."

"I am. What are you looking for, Ava?"

"I'm still figuring that out. I know I want something different than what I had." She tilted her head to see him better. "I've been making a list."

He brushed a curl out of her face. "Of what you're looking for?"

She nodded. "A pros and cons list for what I want, and don't want, in a relationship."

Roman ran his hand down her shoulder. "Would you mind sharing some of it with me?"

"Well…the cons have been easy. I don't want someone who tries to control me, talks down to me, or constantly fights with me. I don't want a relationship that weighs me down with each passing day. And I don't want to be with a man who makes me compromise who I really am."

His arms held her tight. "Those are completely valid points, Ava. What about the positives? The pros?"

"Those have been a bit trickier. Now that Sebastian's presence isn't looming over me, I've been trying to focus on what *I* truly want."

"And that is?"

"Someone thoughtful and generous. A man who cares about people other than himself. Who knows how to have a healthy disagreement and still be respectful. A relationship where my sexual requests are appealing and not offensive. And maybe a relationship that is a little less…conventional than normal. Is that okay?" She squeezed her eyes shut, hoping she didn't overshare.

He kissed the spot above her ear, and she opened her eyes. "Of course that's okay. You deserve all those things and more. In fact, I think you should spend some time with Logan tomorrow."

She tried to sit up, but he held her firm against him. "You want me to go out with Logan? Why?"

"Ava, I'd be a fool not to see there's something happening between you two." When she tensed in his arms, he ran his hand down her side, trying to soothe her with his touch. "I'm not mad about it. In fact, I think you should explore it a bit more."

"That doesn't bother you?"

"Of course it does. I'm crazy about you, if you haven't noticed. I'd rather it be just me making you come night after night." He ran his nose against her hair, breathing in her smell, reveling in the feel of her curls against his face. "But it doesn't make me angry. You've been open about your desires. You played me the voice message. I'm not the kind of man who's going to stand in the way of what you want."

Finally, Ava began to relax once more against him. She tilted back and kissed the underside of his jaw. "And Logan is okay with this?"

"I'd venture to say after tonight, he's more than okay with it."

She squirmed in his arms. "You knew he was in the doorway watching us?"

He nodded against her head.

Her movement stilled. "I'm sorry I didn't say anything."

"Don't apologize. It's confusing for me. I imagine it's confusing for you, too."

"This isn't going to wreck your friendship? I don't want to get in the way of anything."

"We've been friends for almost two decades. There's not a lot we haven't been through together—good and bad."

"How did you two become friends?" Ava played with his fingers, intertwined with hers. "You two couldn't be more different if you tried."

"Logan relocated to Little Greenfield during his last year of high school. He'd already had a rough time with his dad leaving them years earlier. The scumbag racked up a huge gambling debt using Logan's mom's name. She worked multiple jobs for years trying to pay it off and finally couldn't afford to live in Toronto any longer. So Little Greenfield became their new home. A small town has smaller prices."

"I had no idea he went through that."

"There's more to the story, but that's for Logan to tell. And for another time." He cleared his throat. Thinking about what a jag Logan's dad had been—and still was—always made his blood boil. "The kids at school were already in tight-knit groups. We'd been with each other for the past thirteen years, after all. Logan was guarded and sullen, not open to making friends. I sensed that he needed someone and reached out. It took a couple of tries, but eventually, he came around."

"And that was the start of your beautiful friendship?" she teased.

"It was, indeed. We've been best friends ever since."

She batted her long eyelashes at him. "Like a cute married couple."

"Yeah, yeah." He kissed her nose. "We've *been together long enough to be considered common-law*. We're a *bromance*. If we *don't find spouses by the time we're forty, we should marry each other*. We've heard it all."

"So you're comfortable with each other." She said it like a fact, not a question.

"That's right."

"So if I go with Logan tomorrow, you're both okay with it? It's not going to turn into a he-man pissing contest?"

He chuckled. "Not at all, love."

"Thank you, Roman. I don't know what I've done to deserve you."

"I just want you to be happy."

Roman pulled the comforter over them. He settled in with Ava curled snuggly against his chest. This felt right. Natural. Easy. He'd worry about their future after Logan took Ava out tomorrow. Right now, he wanted to be in the moment with Ava.

In his bed.

Together.

Chapter Eleven

LOGAN

Outside the B&B, Logan leaned against his limited edition Rocket 3R. The sun was high in the sky, beating down, warming the leather of his motorcycle's black saddle. He knew he had to be on his A game today. Last night, Roman and Ava had fucked like animals. He'd heard them through his room's closed door, all the way down the hall. And, of course, there was the watching.

That idiot Sebastian had made him so mad, he'd shut off the recording half-way through. The message was a road map to Ava's sexual desires, but he wanted to discover them for himself. After listening to the first half, he understood enough of what she wanted to try. So what if he'd been using it to his advantage?

She liked to watch. She wanted to be watched. A

little voyeuristic fantasy mixed with exhibitionist tendencies. He had no trouble getting on board with that.

Eventually, he'd have to tell her he listened to part of the message. Not before he made his case to her, though. And not before he had a chance to fuck any negative thoughts about him right out of her head.

He could be civilized.

He could be…nice.

He hadn't always been such a stony bastard. Vague memories of being an excitable, friendly young boy came to mind. Sure, he had been a kid, but the memories were there.

When his dad lost their money and left, he'd been eight years old. All he knew was that his mom needed to get another job, so he saw less of her, and his dad wasn't living with them anymore. Months of therapy told him it was normal for him to think he was at fault, even though he wasn't. But Logan wasn't great at therapy—what eight-year-old was?—and the lesson never quite stuck.

He'd spent most of his youth trying to win his father's love. If he tried hard enough, got good enough grades, played the right sports, said the right things, his dad would finally say that he loved him. But his dad's visits and calls became less frequent. Soon he only saw his good-for-nothing dad for a few hours on his birthday or at Christmas, if he was lucky.

Hitting the slots was more important. Losing one more round of blackjack was more important. Taking out another advance on another credit card was more important.

Eventually, his mother shared with him that his dad had a new wife and step-children. Logan and his mom weren't a priority. Not that they had been for a while. He remembered not feeling angry or upset. Rather, he pitied the new family who now had to deal with his gambling addiction and credit card debt.

The year his father forgot to show for his sixteenth birthday was the final nail in the coffin of their relationship. He should have closed the casket and buried it long before that day. But kids are kids, and they have hope.

From that day on, it became easier to guard himself from people. If no one came into his life, then no one had to leave. A simple solution to a complex problem. It wasn't until a decade later that Logan realized how shitty his dad also treated his mother.

Now, twenty years later, he continued to cling on to his simple solution of being an asshole and pushing people away.

He had an inkling that this wasn't working with Ava. Okay, more than an inkling. But it had been years since he let anyone new in.

The front door clicking open and closed grabbed his attention and brought him out of the pity party in his head. Ava was a fucking snack. Short, flowy skirt.

Tight, cropped sweater. Not the best attire for riding on the back of his bike, but he wasn't going to ask her to change. Not when she looked like that. He watched as she scanned the yard, searching. When her gaze landed on him, leaning against his motorbike with an extra helmet propped on the seat, her eyebrows shot up.

"Not afraid of getting on this thing, are you?" he teased, patting the helmet for good measure.

Her posture stiffened a fraction. "Not at all."

He stifled the laugh bubbling up in his throat as she walked over to him, hesitation in each step. "I'm a safe driver, I promise. Roman wouldn't let you ride with me if I wasn't."

"Yeah, that's probably true."

"It is." He handed her the lid and dug a spare leather jacket out of his bike's back compartment. "Put this on too."

"Where are we going?" she asked as she put on the helmet and jacket.

"You'll see." He straddled the bike and motioned to the pillion seat behind him. "Get on." He owed Roman a fucking huge *thank you* for convincing Ava to go with him today.

She awkwardly climbed on behind him, like she was trying not to touch him. Stumbling, she fell against him, one arm bracing herself against his hip.

"Sorry, I didn't mean to do that."

He bet if he could see her face under the helmet,

it would be bright red. A chuckle escaped him, and he shook his head. "Sweetheart, you're going to have to hold on tight, anyway. May as well start now."

Ava settled behind him and hesitantly placed her arms around his torso. He drew her close. The heat of her body radiated up his spine. She was the hottest cling-on he'd ever had on his bike. Her skirt rode up, and the press of her pussy against him was almost enough to do him in. Cancel this stupid bike ride, take her inside, and beg her to let him fuck her six ways from Sunday. But that's not what she needed.

She needed to see he was a good guy.

He could be trusted.

He could satisfy her.

He could not be an asshole. Maybe.

The backroads behind the bed and breakfast were long, winding, and scenic. Ava's arms wrapped around him, holding him close, made him feel more invincible. It felt right having her snug against him on the back of his ride.

They arrived at a modern-looking building, no larger than a single-family bungalow, and Logan helped Ava off his bike.

"What is this place?" Ava took in her surroundings with admiration.

"A craft gin distillery. Gertie's grandson, Jack, just

finished getting it up and running. We're going to be the first to try his stock."

Ava clutched his arm. "This is amazing! How did you know I love gin?"

"A hunch." He winked at her, loving that she was clinging on to his arm. Twenty minutes on his bike with her arms wrapped around him had broken down any lingering fear of being close to him. Another reason to love his ride.

Her eyebrows knitted together. "No, seriously. How did you know?"

He shrugged. "I didn't. But I thought you'd appreciate the experience regardless of if you were a fan of gin."

She laughed. "So you lucked out."

"I guess you could say that."

"Holy smokes, there you are!" Jack called out, strolling down the front steps of the building. "I've been waiting for ya. Welcome to Jack and Jill's Gin Distillery. What took ya so long?" He shook both their hands and invited them inside.

"We took the scenic route. I wanted to give Ava a ride to remember."

"Well, nothing wrong with that." He clapped Logan on the back and ushered them along. "Let me give you the tour." He directed their attention as they walked, and he talked. "These are our mash cookers. Those"—he pointed—"are our stills. And that area houses our spirit safes and receiver tanks."

All the equipment was new and shone in the light from the windows on the sides of the building. Copper and hammered metal complemented each other perfectly. Jack had done a great job making the space clean and stylish. Logan appreciated the little touches, like the matching copper tasting tables and brushed nickel bar. He appreciated it even more with Ava's hand still clutching his bicep.

"This is perfect timing." Jack beamed from ear to ear. "When Grandma Gertie called and said you wanted a tour, I got so excited. We just finished distilling our first three batches of product. Getting you to taste it is gonna be the highlight of my week."

"Thank you for letting us be your first customers," Ava said.

"Even if we hate the gin, we'll tell you we love it," Logan joked.

"Oh, come now." Jack slapped Logan on the shoulder. "You're gonna love it, I promise."

They sat on the wooden stools in front of the tasting table while Jack poured three different gins into shot glasses. He set the bottles behind each different gin so they could see what they were drinking. Logan admired the muted colours and simple design of the labels. Jack really had his shit figured out.

"These are stunning," Ava commented, taking the one with the violet label and turning it in her hands. "Did you design them?"

"Oh, heaven's no. That would be my wonderful wife, Emma. She's a graphic designer."

"Well she does incredible work. You should both be proud."

Jack beamed. "Thank you, Ava. I'll make sure to pass along your kind words."

During the tasting, Jack was a complete professional. Always offering Ava the sample first, then Logan. Telling them the notes of each, and how he and his business partner, Jill, invented the flavour profiles.

"I think the saskatoon berry flavour is my favourite," Ava said, licking the last drop off the rim of the glass.

It took everything in him to not lean forward and taste the gin lingering on her tongue.

"What about you, Logan?" Jack asked, breaking the spell Ava's mouth had cast on him.

"The Gin Rummy, easy. Love the mix of rum and gin. Great notes of cinnamon and ginger. And it's a clever name." He ran a palm down Ava's back, testing the waters. She leaned into his touch, so he let his hand rest above her ass. Fuck, her body felt good.

"But the honey and violet flavour was good, too." She gave a reassuring touch on Jack's forearm. "You knocked it out of the park, Jack. Truly."

Logan nodded in agreement.

"Thank you so much, you two. You've really buoyed my confidence. We knew we had something special here, but of course we're partial to our own product. Let me mix you both a G&T and I'll take you out back to our patio."

"I'm good, thanks. Still need to drive home. But I'm sure Ava would love one." He slipped a finger beneath the waistband of her skirt, gently grazing her bare skin.

She placed her hand on his thigh. "Yes, please. With the saskatoon berry gin, if you don't mind."

Jack mixed her gin and tonic, then led them out back, where a handful of wrought-iron tables sat in a beautifully landscaped garden, then left them alone to continue their date.

"This place is wonderful," Ava mused, sipping her cocktail.

"Little Greenfield is small," Logan said. "But Roman and I have done our research, and we think it's going to be an up-and-coming town. Places like this"—he gestured to the distillery—"are opening not-too-far from our B&B, and they're a major draw for tourists. We have great local shops on Main Street, and Kawawaymog Lake is magnificent any time of year. I think we're about to see a large influx of tourists."

"I was wondering why you were building a B&B. Does Little Greenfield get many visitors? Besides the fishing competition." Her pink lips wrapped around the edge of her coupe glass.

God, she was a picture of perfection.

"Not an overwhelming amount, but they'll come. With proper advertising, which I've talked to the town council about, I know we can draw some good crowds."

This was going well. He was talking to her like a normal human, not an emotionally unavailable man. And she was responding. Progress.

But he needed to find out if she was into him. He had Roman to compete with, after all. Time to raise the intensity.

Logan grabbed the leg of Ava's chair and dragged her beside him in one swift motion. He didn't miss the unmistakable heat in her eyes. Only for a second, but he saw it. "Tell me more about you, Ava. We haven't had the chance to talk."

"Are you kidding? Yes, we have. You didn't want to get to know me." She cocked an eyebrow, drilling him with her stare.

He threw up his hands in mock surrender. "True. But you've been so preoccupied with Roman."

Ava poked his chest. "Not an excuse. You've been haughty since the moment you saw me."

"There's a good reason."

She pursed her lips. "Why do I doubt that?"

Okay. Perhaps this wasn't going as smoothly as he initially thought.

"Do you want an honest answer?"

She leaned toward him. "If you're willing to give it."

"I was angry Roman met you first." There. His feelings were out in the open.

Ava's forehead scrunched. "What? Why?"

He shouldn't have rolled his eyes, but he did. "Sweetheart, the instant I laid eyes on you, I wanted to fuck you."

Too honest?

Ava froze with her mouth agape. She sat unmoving for what felt like forever. "I thought you didn't even like me," she finally said.

"Does this look like I don't like you?" He gestured under the table to where his cock was straining against his jeans.

Her lips parted.

The entire ride here, he was aroused by the feel of her pressed flush against him. Then the subtle touches during the gin tasting, and now her sitting right next to him, smelling of lavender and spirits. He couldn't contain himself. His hard-on ached for contact. Whether it would be from her or his own hand, he didn't know. But he sincerely fucking hoped it was the former.

Logan's lips burned with the need to finally kiss her. Yeah, she felt something too. He recognized it in her eyes, in the way she held her breath when she glanced at him, and how she'd slightly parted her legs when he'd pulled her chair closer.

Leaning forward, he brushed his nose against her cheek. "Let's get out of here."

She touched her throat. "Logan, I don't know, I—"

"Don't say anything else." He stood and peered in the door, calling out a *goodbye* to Jack. Turning back to Ava, he made a simple demand. "Get on my bike." He knew from Sebastian's ridiculous message that she liked to be bossed around—dominated, even—when the act was consensual.

Ava dutifully followed him to his ride without another word, and they climbed on. He took her arms and wrapped them tightly around his waist. His cock was throbbing, but he could wait.

She had to make the first move.

She had to want this, too.

He tore out of the distillery's dirt parking lot and headed the opposite way home. The short way. No chance in hell he was taking the scenic route this time. He wanted—no, needed—to get Ava home on the off chance she wanted to explore things with him.

All he needed was a sign. One sign. One show of interest.

The bike rumbled between his legs as he raced to the bed and breakfast, itching to ignore the speed limit signs, but not willing to put Ava in any unnecessary danger.

Her arms were snug around his hips. When did she lower them? Her warmth radiated through his leather jacket and into his body. Each minute shift made him more feral.

The sensation of something skimming his jeans snared his attention. He spared a glance down and saw Ava's hand resting on his leg.

Until now, he'd never uttered a prayer in his life. But he prayed she'd put her hand exactly where he wanted it. He begged all the gods to grant him this one thing.

Her palm slid higher on his inner thigh until it landed on his cock. She groped him through his jeans, exploring his length.

Fuck yes.

He hauled ass the rest of the way home.

Chapter Twelve

AVA

What was she doing? Ava peeled herself off of Logan's motorcycle, discarding the helmet and jacket, and headed for the door. Logan followed behind her. What was this heat crackling in the air between them? Was it real, or nerves, or something else?

He'd been a completely different person today. A better version of himself. More open, less of a scoundrel—though he still had the same smug attitude she'd come to know this past week. But now she viewed it more as arrogant confidence than self-righteousness.

She couldn't deny the electricity she felt the other night when he stood in the doorway watching Roman and her. Thinking she could have two men was foolish, though, wasn't it? Even if Roman said he wouldn't stand in their way. Logan had been nothing but a hostile version of amicable toward her until today. Yet she couldn't help the way her pulse skyrocketed when she groped him on his motorcycle. Him in that leather jacket, riding the sexiest motorcycle she'd ever seen, after he admitted he wanted to fuck her? All too tempting.

Her breath quickened as he trailed behind her to the front entrance.

Making way for Logan to enter first, she stepped to the side. Instead of letting them in, Logan drew nearer, snaking his arm around her waist.

"Did you like it when I watched the other night?" His mouth was dangerously close to hers.

Her heart was beating out of her chest. "Y-yes," she stammered. No point in lying. The exhibition she put on was proof enough that she liked it.

His arm tightened around her. "Did you like how I touched myself to the sight of you?"

Barely audible, she murmured, "Yes."

Guiding her toward the entrance, he continued, "I think it's only fair that you get the full experience. Roman got to have you." He surrounded her, and threw open the door. "Now it's my turn."

Her head was spinning. Logan's body against hers was making her weak in the knees.

Pushing her inside, Logan slammed the door shut and shoved her against it. His rough hands grabbed her sides, cupped her breasts, and tangled in her hair.

"Tell me you don't want this and I'll stop."

"I..." She did want this. That was the problem. She wanted what she had with Roman, but deep down, she also wanted to explore what Logan offered. Ava sensed it would be different. Harder. Rougher. But that was madness. Nobody got to have two men. Choices needed to be made, and Logan had been nothing but a brooding asshole since she arrived. A sexy, brooding asshole, but an asshole.

"I don't want to wreck what I have with Roman."

A deep chuckle left Logan's throat. It sounded dangerous coming from him, normally so humourless.

He tugged her hair at the roots and angled her head so she had no choice but to look him in the eye. "Sweetheart, what did he say about me taking you out today?"

Gathering her thoughts, she managed to squeak out, "He won't get in the way of anything."

Logan bent down and put his face so close to hers, their noses touched. His warm breath cascaded across her skin, the scent of leather filled her senses. "This was Roman's idea."

Now that she was actually with Logan, his breath in her ear, his words hit her like a freight train. Roman was okay with this. Logan seemed okay with this. They had talked about this happening.

Ava's racing thoughts were ceased by Logan's

fingers tracing along the inside of her thigh, stopping right below the hem of her skirt. Suddenly, she couldn't remember what she'd been thinking about. She only cared about the fingertips caressing her delicate skin, making her pussy clench, making her wet.

"I know you want this," he whispered, his hand ghosting further up her thigh. "We can figure out the rest later."

She definitely wanted it. The heat between them was real. She sensed it from day one, but it seemed like annoyance on his end. Loathing even.

"I need you so bad, sweetheart, it's driving me insane. But this is your choice. I'll stop right now if you say the word."

The words left her lips before she could overthink her decision. "Don't stop."

His mouth crashed against hers, igniting her desire. The hand that was skimming her thigh moved higher, cupping her pussy roughly. She let out a quiet moan. This was crossing a line. It had to be.

"You need to get out of your head, Ava," Logan said in her ear. "Let me help."

Strong hands grasped her hips and lifted her against his body. Logan stalked confidently to one of the wooden dining tables and placed her in front of it. Spinning her around, he set his palm on her back and forcefully pushed her chest down onto the table. He used his leg to kick apart her feet so she was spread in front of him, skirt riding up her back.

"I'm going to fuck you hard and use you how I want. I'm going to make you a slut for my cock. Does that sound good to you?"

She nodded her head against the table. The unmistakable sound of a belt being undone came from behind her, followed by the rustle of his jeans.

"I'm going to need to hear it from your mouth, Ava. Say it so I can hear it."

She inhaled deeply and let herself say the words. "I want that. I want you to use me."

"So desperate for me." He clicked his tongue. "Hands on the table."

She obeyed and Logan dug his fingers into her hair, grasping it close to the scalp. He pulled back firmly, jerking her head off the table. With his other hand, he wrenched her thong down her thighs and left it stretched between her knees.

"Fuck, Ava. Red as sin. Did you wear that for me?"

"Yes," she answered, and an agonizing moan left Logan's lips. "I figured since you liked my pink one so much, I'd wear this for you today. Even if you never got to see it."

He leaned in closer, and the familiar rip of a condom wrapper was followed by a puff of air leaving Logan's lips, which sent the top of the wrapper floating down on the table.

"No," she said. "We don't need it."

He notched his cock at her entrance, and her legs began to tremble. "Are you sure?"

"Very." She wanted to turn around and see him. See the expression on his face, see how he looked at her in this moment. But his grip on her hair was tight and punishing. Logan was in control.

"Normally, I'd want to take my time with you. Make you squirm until you beg for me to fuck your needy cunt."

He pressed into her, and she tried to stifle her gasp. Her pussy desperately tried to stretch to accommodate the sudden intrusion of him.

Logan let out a groan. If she wasn't already dripping for him, that would've done it. She loved a vocal man in the bedroom. Or in this case, the dining room.

"But you've been teasing me all week," he crooned in her ear. "So I'm gonna fuck you like the tease you are."

He pulled out and drove back into her, pumping at a demanding pace. One hand on her hip, the other gripped tight to her hair. It forced her to arch her back, creating the perfect angle for him to hit that spot inside that made her lose control.

A sharp smack to the side of her ass sent goosebumps across her skin. A second spank in the same spot had her moaning. A third had her crying out, "More."

More of everything.

"I'll decide what you get more of, sweetheart."

Logan's fingers soothed the sting with a brief rub before tugging her hair and wrenching her flush against his front. Her back to his chest. He pumped in and out of her, not missing a beat. The wet sounds vulgar in the quiet air of the cabin.

His hand snaked from her hair to wrap around her waist possessively. She mourned the loss of the stinging sensation on her scalp. She ached for his punishing touch. If not wrapped in her hair, then somewhere else. Anywhere else, as long as he was touching her.

"Please," she whimpered, barely audible over their heavy breathing.

"Please what?" he growled in her ear.

"Please touch me." Her voice was a whisper. The harsh pump of his cock inside her was making her unravel.

His free hand lifted the front of her skirt, and his middle finger slipped between her folds. It grazed against her clit, drawing perfect circles. Her whole body shivered in response.

"Such a needy little slut." Pulling his finger away, he held it in front of her face. "Taste," he commanded.

She eagerly opened her mouth and accepted his finger, sucking her own wetness off his skin. He yanked free of her mouth and craned her head to the side. His lips met hers in a brutal kiss, tongue invading, opening her deeper to him. A low groan rose in his throat.

"Fuck, Ava," he panted, drawing back. "You taste so good."

His fingers went to work on her clit again while his cock drove into her from behind. A piercing slap to her clit rocked her entire body. Her inner walls started to spasm.

"Come on my cock, sweetheart," Logan moaned in her ear. "I wanna feel you shatter in my arms."

Another sharp slap to her now overly-sensitive clit sent her racing toward her orgasm. Logan's teeth nipped the side of her neck while he slapped her clit one last time. She erupted in wave after wave of hot pleasure. Logan's movements shuddered and slowed as he climaxed alongside her.

Their ragged breathing was the only sound in the silent air of the cabin. Logan removed himself from her pussy and flipped her to face him.

Then he was descending on her, kissing her, moaning into her mouth. His tongue met her own, swirling around in a heated dance. His hands were in her hair, on her back, squeezing her breasts. He was everywhere at once.

"I want more of you," he grunted, shoving two fingers inside her aching cunt, slick with his cum.

Ava gasped. She was sore, but the intrusion was such a good hurt, she welcomed it. He pushed in a third, drawing his fingers up and in, up and in. Over and over. Her head was spinning.

"Do you want more, little whore?" His voice was dark and wild. The sound of thinly veiled restraint.

How did he know what to say to her? How to stimulate her just right? It's like he was inside her head.

"God, yes," Ava cried out, riding his fingers now as he worked them inside her. "I want more. I want you."

Of course she did. How could she not? She wanted him to edge her until she was a blubbering mess. She wanted him to take control of her body. She wanted him everywhere, in every way, punishing her with his touch.

"Thank fuck," he breathed, dragging his fingers out from inside her. He threw her over his shoulder and made his way to the secret door at the back of the kitchen. "I'm only getting started."

Chapter Thirteen

LOGAN

Ava laid on his bed, head hanging off the side. His cock was buried in her throat as he fucked her face. She gagged and drooled and, he knew, loved each second. His mind reeled with the ways he could make her come.

Her naked body was spread out on the bed before him. She was perfect. Her tits were bouncing from the force of his cock driving into her mouth. She had one arm wrapped around his hips, digging her nails into his ass cheek. The other was on her clit, playing with herself as he drove his dick mercilessly into her throat.

Her legs were spread wide open, and all he could think about was how much he wanted to bury his face between them and eat her cunt like it was his last meal. He needed to taste it. Just the thought had him spilling down her throat. She coughed and gagged, then swallowed around him.

"Such a good fucking girl."

By the end of the night, he would own her every possible way.

It was impossible to wait any longer. He withdrew from her mouth and circled to the other side of the bed. Gripping her legs, he hauled her right to the edge and situated himself between her thighs.

He gave her cunt one long, languid lick. "Fuck, sweetheart. I could eat you all day. Tell me to keep going."

"Keep going," she whimpered. "Please keep going."

Logan dragged his tongue across her pussy, dipping inside her, licking to her clit where he sucked and nipped. He held his tongue firm and moved it quickly across the sensitive point. Her thighs gripped his head tightly, and he could feel her back arching.

Prying her thighs loose, he spread her wide open, his tongue continuing to work her over. He pushed two fingers inside her, rubbing her g-spot fervently. She squirmed on the bed, breathy little moans quickly turning into screams of pleasure.

"You're so wet for me," he panted against her cunt, eating it like the sweet treat it was.

She pulsed against his fingers, and he pressed harder while keeping the same rhythm, and she cried out. Her body tensed against his, and he kept going.

Warmth flooded his face and hand. He tasted it while licking her pussy, savouring the warmth of her squirting on his face.

"My wet slut. You're a masterpiece." His chin dripped with her arousal.

"It's all you." Her voice shook, and she went slack with her most recent release.

He'd never been with a girl who could squirt before. No doubt in his mind—he needed to make her do that again. Feel it drip down his thighs.

Opening the drawer of his nightstand, he retrieved a bottle of lube, a silk tie, and a little surprise he'd bought earlier in the week on his excursion to Ottawa to steal Sebastian's hat. In case something like this happened.

"Roll over, Ava," he commanded. "Ass up."

In the afterglow of her second orgasm, she obliged without question, rolling onto her hands and knees so her perfectly shaped ass was in the air. God, he loved that ass. Thick and full. Exactly what he craved.

He spread her cheeks, giving her tight asshole a quick lick. Ava gasped and glanced at him, a question in her eye.

"You want this?" he asked, giving her an easy out. She could say no; he wouldn't fault her for it.

Slowly, she nodded. "So much."

"Have you had it here before?"

She shook her head. "Only with my toys."

The thought of Ava using a plug or dildo on herself, stretching her ass, making it ready, got him hard once more and heavy with need. He put the silk tie in her mouth and tied it tight behind her head, using it as a gag.

"If it's too much, you tap twice. Either on me or on the bed." He demonstrated, tapping her twice on the arm and tapping twice on the bed. "Understand?"

She nodded again, hunger in her eyes. She was clearly excited, and that made him excited.

"Show me."

She signaled as he said, tapping twice on the bed. Good. No confusion about stopping if needed.

Resuming his position behind Ava, he opened the bottle of lube and poured a generous amount on her backside. He added some to his finger and gently worked his way inside her hole.

"Breathe out. Relax."

Ava groaned against her gag, head down against the mattress.

"You good?" he asked.

She nodded, keeping her breathing steady.

Logan grabbed the surprise he bought earlier in the week. Although he wasn't sure he'd get to use it on her, he thought he'd take a chance. He was glad he did.

He clicked on the small but powerful bullet vibrator, circled his arm around Ava, and placed it gently against her clit. She immediately moaned and bucked against his hand.

Good. He needed her to be as ready as possible.

He worked the bullet against her clit while working a second finger inside her ass. Then a third. Stretching her slowly, preparing her to take every inch of him.

She was a needy mess, writhing on the bed, breathing hard against the makeshift gag, desperate for more. Whenever she got close to climaxing, he jerked the vibrator away. There was no way he'd let her climax without him inside her.

Logan got himself ready. Stroking his cock base to tip with the lube. His body shuddered in anticipation. He couldn't wait to be inside her, having her ass grip his cock tight. Spreading her cheeks, he set his tip against her asshole, slowly pushing in.

"Two taps, remember. But you're going to do your best to take my dick like a good girl." She responded so well when he gave it to her rough and hard, but he was always slow and gentle at the start of this process. Before he really got going, she needed to adjust.

She nodded again, whimpering into the sheets, fisting them with her hands.

He added more lube, then pushed in deeper. For all that was holy, he wanted to slam right home. "You're so tight," he moaned.

Her ass eagerly accepted him. Finally, he was seated inside her to the base of his cock. He took a second to bend over her and drag his tongue along her spine.

Inch by inch, he rocked in and out, until the motion was easy and fluid. Ava pressed against him, silently begging for more. The time for being gentle was done.

Logan wanted her dripping everywhere by the end of this.

His grip on Ava's hip turned punishing. He yanked her against himself again and again, rocking into her, his own orgasm climbing rapidly. He wouldn't come before feeling her squirt again.

He pulled out and laid down face-up next to Ava on the bed. A whine escaped her lips as she lost contact with him and the vibrator.

"Get on top," he ordered. "I need you to soak me while my cock is in your ass."

Ava quickly obliged, straddling his hips. He saw the same hunger he experienced mirrored in her eyes. Logan took in her form while she lowered herself onto him once more. The curve of her hips, the slight waist, the heavy handful of tits. Her cheeks were flushed, her lips full and swollen from earlier. He'd never seen a more beautiful sight in all his life. In this instant, she was his perfect slutty toy.

A moan escaped Ava's lips around the makeshift gag and brought him back to himself. She was working herself up and down his shaft, hands braced against his chest.

His orgasm was threatening to explode once again, but he needed to feel Ava come on him. Needed it like the air he breathed.

Pressing the bullet vibrator to her clit once more, she began to buck against him. "Look at you, Ava. My filthy little slut," he groaned out between gritted teeth. "Come on me. Soak me. We're not done here until your arousal fucking drenches me."

Her release flowed out of her on his last word. Warm and wet, coating the base of his cock, spreading to his hips, and dripping onto the sheets below him. She cried out against the gag, and the sound of her voice shot straight to his cock, pushing him over the edge. He let loose inside her ass, filling her with his cum.

Ava didn't relent. She kept riding him, slowly, as he orgasmed. A guttural sound poured from his clenched teeth as he kept coming.

Never in his life had he experienced a climax so long or so intense.

He sat up to meet Ava, still straddling him, and circled his arms around her waist, pressing his face against her breasts. He breathed in and out slowly, trying to calm his racing heart. Reaching up, he untied her gag and let it fall on the sheets, then placed his arms back around her.

Gentle lips pressed against the top of his head. Ava rained slow, sensual kisses anywhere she could reach while he collected himself. He should be taking care of her, comforting her, not the other way around. But something about her broke through his barriers. He'd let loose with her tonight. Trusted her to take it.

And if he could trust her with this, couldn't he trust her to be there for him in other ways? As someone to talk to, someone to support him, someone to be his person?

How was this going to work? The obvious chemistry between her and Roman was something special. Where did he fit in? Logan didn't want this to be a one-time fuck. Initially, that's what he wanted. But sometime this past week, something changed.

Maybe it was her so freely helping them out with the bed and breakfast. Never complaining, always ready for the next task.

Maybe it was her confidence and ability to meet him head on. It took her but a couple days to not tolerate his bullshit. The way she challenged him after he brought her that douchebag's hat was remarkable.

Maybe it was just her.

Whatever it was? He needed to hold on to it. The three of them had to figure this out, because he wasn't letting go.

Chapter Fourteen

AVA

She sat in the living area, buttoning and unbuttoning the top of her floral blouse. Ink stained her left palm from her quick scrawls of *confidence, subtle touches,* and *ass-play* on her relationships pro list at two in the morning. She'd scraped her hand through her hair so many times already, her curls were probably completely frazzled. Yeah, like ink stains and frizzy hair were her biggest problems right now. If only.

Last night was…there were no words. Logan left her speechless. They'd fucked until the early morning hours. Afterward, he'd taken care of her in such an intimate way that the mere thought of it made her stomach flutter.

He washed her body in the shower, lavishing her

skin with his lips. Taking his time, he ran a towel across her. Drying her gently. Then he walked her to her bedroom and said goodnight with one of the most passionate kisses she'd ever experienced.

He'd invited her to stay in his room, sleep in his bed with him. But she couldn't do that to Roman. Not when she didn't know what the hell was going to happen between them all.

She laughed at herself. Like sleeping in Logan's bed would be the thing that upset Roman. Like she didn't just spend the night getting royally fucked and dominated by his best friend. Between the night with Logan and the previous night with Roman, she was beyond sore. The ache between her thighs was a severe reminder that the three of them needed to slow down and have a serious talk.

Which was why she'd been lingering in the living room since six in the morning, waiting for them both to start the day. Now the time read 7:02, and she swore she'd burned a few hundred calories from the amount of pacing and fidgeting she'd done.

When the concealed panel to the back house finally opened, and Roman and Logan walked in together, she let out a relieved sigh. They hadn't killed each other. No one had a black eye or a busted jaw. No blood on them or their clothing.

Good.

That was a start.

"Morning," she called, drawing their attention to her.

"Morning, love." Roman sat close to her on the couch and placed a soft kiss against her lips.

Logan gave her a curt nod and joined them in the living room, hovering near the fireplace. He refused to make eye contact.

Great.

"So…" She cleared her throat. "We need to talk. All of us."

Logan grunted his agreement, and Roman squeezed her knee.

"I'm going to be honest. I don't know what's happening between the three of us." She turned toward Roman. "I slept with Logan last night."

"I know." The low vibration of his voice rumbled in the air.

"And how do you feel about that?"

"Well…" He rubbed the back of his neck. "Being with him was my idea in the first place, wasn't it? So while I'd love to keep you to myself, I'd be an idiot not to acknowledge the sparks flying between you two."

She glanced at Logan. His face was a picture of composure with no discernible emotion or reaction to what they were saying.

"Logan—how do you feel about me being with Roman?"

"I'd rather it be only me fucking you, but I know that's not what you want."

Ava nodded, her knee bouncing. She placed her hand on it to steady the motion, but it didn't help.

"Where do we go from here? Is this a one-time thing between us or—?"

"No," they both barked out.

Her head jerked back. "So you're both cool with this?"

"I wouldn't say he's *cool* with it." Roman flicked his thumb in Logan's direction. "But he's coming around. He said he'd be willing to try."

"Try? Try what? Did you already talk about this without me?"

Roman took her hands in his, and her leg stopped bouncing. Her body calmed when he touched her.

"We had a chat this morning—man-to-man—about what we're open to." Roman gave Logan a pointed stare.

"And," Logan chimed in. "We're willing to try out a poly situation, if that's what you want. As long as I don't have to touch Roman's dick."

Roman laughed as he gestured to his well-toned body. "You wish you could get a piece of this."

Logan rolled his eyes. "I'm good, thanks."

Roman wiggled his eyebrows at him. "Aw, come on, buddy. I'd touch your dick if Ava wanted me to. You're a handsome man. I don't discriminate."

"Stay away from my dick, Banks."

"Okay, okay," Ava interjected, a nervous laugh

escaping her. "You're saying I can be with both of you? Neither of you are mad?"

Roman cupped her cheek. "I think we have a lot to figure out—but no, love, we aren't mad."

"This all happened so fast. I don't expect you both to automatically be alright with this. I'm certainly not an expert on this."

"We'll figure it out together." Roman's reassuring tone was exactly what she needed to hear. "Who cares that it happened quickly? I think there was a reason you ended up in Little Greenfield. With us." He shared a poignant look with Logan.

"Roman's right. We won't know if it works unless we try. And…" He blew out the word with a long breath. "If I have to share you with someone, I'm glad it's Roman."

Roman's grin was so big, it had to have been hurting his face. "Oh, I'm sorry. I didn't quite get that last bit. Can you say it again?"

"I will not."

"Come here, Logey. Join the throuple." Roman snorted, wrapping his arms around Ava. "Tell us more about how much you love me."

"We are not calling ourselves a throuple." His tone was dead serious.

Ava giggled. "Is it too late to back out of this?"

"Yes," both men said, not missing a beat.

ROMAN

Ava had been with them for eight days now. The last two days had been spent navigating the newness of their relationship as a triad. Logan didn't like labels, and hated when he called them that, but that's what they were.

Everything was going smoothly. Well, as smoothly as one could expect when dating the same woman as their best friend while living in the same house. Truth be told, the situation was easier than he thought. He really didn't mind seeing Logan and Ava together. It made him happy to see her happy.

Logan, on the other hand, was taking it as expected. But only a couple of days had passed since they officially decided to both be with Ava. Eventually, Logan would get used to it and not be as jealous. Though he doubted the jealousy would ever fully go away. Logan let too few people in and was too possessive for that.

"Earth to Roman." Ava waved a hammer in front of his face. "Did you hear me?"

Logan snickered from where he was finishing the plumbing in the final guest bathroom.

"Sorry, love. Lost in thought. What did you say?"

"I need you to shine the laser level on the wall behind the bed so I can install the hooks for the paintings."

"Right. Give me a second." He busied himself

adjusting the tripod, so the laser projected on the wall at the right height.

They'd bought the art together—along with Logan—earlier today at a farmer's market in Huntsville. Jamie didn't mind covering his shift at the pub. She'd picked two mixed media pieces of the landscape of south-central Ontario. One featured a whisky jack, the other a white-tailed deer. They were well-suited to the bedroom. She had quite the eye for design, similar to Logan.

When he asked her about it, she said her affinity for design probably came from being around her dad's build sites all the time while growing up. She always jumped at the chance to talk to the owners about their visions for the homes. Sometimes, she got to meet the interior designers if the owners brought them in early.

Logan exited the bathroom and dusted off his hands. "That's the last one. Everything's connected and operational." Leaning against the wall, he watched Ava climb the ladder and nail a picture hook into the wall along the bright red line of the level.

"And after I finish hanging these"—Ava gestured to the art lying on the bed—"this suite will be completed. And you were worried having me here would be a distraction." She clicked her tongue at Logan, feigning disappointment.

Logan walked over, wrapped his arms around her, and scooped her off the ladder. "You are a distraction.

Just in other ways." His palm snaked down her midriff to cup the crotch of the work pants she'd borrowed from him.

Ava angled her head back and kissed him. Deeply. Almost like they forgot Roman was in the room with them. He cleared his throat.

"You want to join?" Ava asked, a playful challenge in her voice.

He raised his eyebrow. "You know I would."

"Pass." Logan broke away from Ava and grabbed the second painting. "I don't want your giant mitts on me."

Roman let out a chuckle and shook his head. One of these days, Logan would lighten up. Either that or he'd be so turned on, he wouldn't say no to all three of them together at the same time. Roman and Ava sometimes talked about it late at night in his bed. It didn't bother him one way or the other, and she wondered what it would be like.

He strode over to Ava and lifted her into his arms. The feel of her legs wrapped around his waist was quickly becoming one of his favourite sensations. His mouth was on hers, his tongue sliding between her lips to find her own. A moan escaped her and sent a spike of desire straight through him. Her hips shifted against his torso, her hands found his hair, her nails scratched at his neck. God, this woman. Everything she did drove him wild.

"Let's go to my room, love. Let me tie you down and fuck you like you need."

"Let's get these hung so we can be finished instead," Logan said from behind them.

Ava snickered and unwrapped her legs. When he gently set her down, she gave him a coy wink. "Another time, big boy."

"Better be soon," he teased, unabashedly palming his erection in front of her.

Ava's phone rang, and she hurried to grab it. When she saw the caller ID, the worry in her expression quickly sobered his mood.

"Who is it?"

"My work. It's my boss. I need to take this." She answered with a concerned *hello* as she left the room.

Logan crossed to him. "That was strange, don't you think?"

"She's been away from work for a while. Maybe her boss is calling to check on her? She *is* supposed to return in two days."

Logan rolled his eyes. "You actually think that's the reason?"

"Why not? That's what I'd be doing if Jamie or Megan were out of the pub for that long."

"Yeah, but we don't know what her boss is like. You're a good guy. Maybe he's not," Logan pointed out.

"Was that a compliment, Logey?"

Logan sighed heavily, but there was amusement in his eyes. "Don't get used to it."

"Are we going to talk to her about when she's coming back?" Roman's chest tightened at the idea of her leaving in two days. They'd been ignoring it until this point, but a call from her boss brought reality to the forefront of his mind. She had a life in Ottawa.

He sighed. "We're running out of time. Let's do it tonight."

Roman nodded. "Alright. Finish hanging those pictures. I want to get a bonfire started for Ava before it gets too late. Then we can all figure this out."

Without complaint, Logan hung the two paintings, and made sure they were level. If it involved doing something for Ava, Logan was on it right away. Roman tidied the supplies and put the ladder away in the hallway storage closet.

"Roman? Logan?" Ava called from downstairs. Her voice sounded pinched and an octave too high.

Logan and he exchanged a worried glance, then raced downstairs to see Ava standing in the middle of the living room, phone hanging at her side in her hand.

"I think I'm in trouble."

Chapter Fifteen

LOGAN

"What did your boss say?" If another jackass mouthed off to Ava, he was going to track him down and glue his lips together. He found Sebastian. He could find her boss.

"I need to go home. Tomorrow." Ava sat on the couch, shoulders slumped and gaze on the floor.

"Tomorrow?" Logan shook his head. "Is there even a plane leaving Little Greenfield tomorrow?"

"Do you want me to check?" Roman asked.

When she nodded, Roman stepped outside—with a reluctant expression on his face—to call Jerry, a close friend and pilot at the one-runway airport.

"What am I going to do?" She stared up at Logan, tears forming in her eyes.

Shit. He wasn't good at comforting people. That was Roman's forte. But this was Ava.

"I was supposed to have two more days off."

He took a seat beside her. "It can't be that bad. Perhaps they just need you back earlier than expected."

"Then why wouldn't he tell me that over the phone?"

"Tell me what he said, specifically."

She took a few shuddering breaths, obviously trying to calm herself. "He said I needed to return as soon as possible, preferably tomorrow. When I asked why, he said it would be better to talk face-to-face because didn't want to give me any details on the phone. He didn't sound pleased."

Logan's face tightened, but he did his best not to frown. No need to cause further alarm. "Let's not panic before we have all the information. It could be many things."

Ava sniffled and Logan felt a piece of his heart break. That was a new sensation. How did he come to care so much for her in such a short time?

He pulled her into his arms and held her tight. "You'll get through this. You have me. And Roman."

She shook her head against his chest. "I was supposed to have two more days here. This is the last night I get to be with you both…" she trailed off, seemingly lost in a memory he didn't have access to.

"It's not the *last* night. You'll be ba—"

Before Logan could get Ava to finish her thought, Roman burst through the door, holding up his phone. "I've convinced Jerry to fly Ava home tomorrow. I owe him a month's worth of free drinks at the pub, but he'll do it."

Roman to the rescue. Though, Logan didn't want Ava to be rescued. He wanted her to stay with them in Little Greenfield. He silently cursed Jerry for being such an agreeable man. The pilot was always more than happy to help the people of Little Greenfield. Why would Ava be any different?

She pulled away from him and went to Roman, who wrapped her in his arms.

"Everything's going to be fine." Roman stroked her hair. "Jerry will take you back first thing in the morning. Work will get sorted out."

"We'll go with you," Logan found himself saying.

"Anything you want, Ava. Would you like us to go, too?"

"I appreciate the offer, but I think I need to handle this on my own. I've jotted down enough positives and negatives on my list, and spent enough time with you both, to know what I deserve. It's time I dealt with the entire mess."

Roman ran the back of his hand down her cheek. "If you're sure, love."

"I am." She sniffed and wiped her eyes with the sleeve of her sweater. "Plus, it's been eight days. The voice message should be old news to everybody by now, right?"

Roman nodded, ever the comforter. Logan knew better. Salacious gossip, like the information Sebastian spread, didn't go away quickly. And Ava leaving immediately after probably added to the fire he caused. Logan wished he'd burst the self-righteous dick-weasel's tires alongside keying his car.

"I should pack my things." Ava trudged up the stairs and into her room.

Logan narrowed his eyes at Roman. "Aren't you going after her?"

He shook his head. "She needs time to think. Let's give her some space and—unless she comes to us—we'll talk to her in the morning."

Shit. Roman was probably right. What could they do for her right now, anyway? Logan started pacing the room, needing to release the negative energy building inside him. Roman watched him, probably trying to gauge how upset he was.

Logan stopped directly in front of him. "She said this is the last night she gets to be with us."

"Well, it is."

He let out a sigh heavy with frustration. "Obviously. But her tone suggested she was more than stating a fact. Almost like she didn't think she'd be coming back."

"Why wouldn't she come back?"

"I don't know, Roman! You burst through the door playing the hero before I asked her."

Roman placed a calming hand on Logan's shoulder. "That doesn't make sense."

"She has a life in Ottawa. We were just a pit stop. You heard the recording. We're two guys to use and abuse." As he said the words, he knew they weren't true. And he regretted them immediately.

Roman raised his eyebrows. "Logan, don't start spiraling because of one off-hand comment. You do this to the people you care about. A hard situation can put you on the defense."

He glared at Roman. Damn him for knowing him so well.

"You know I'm right."

"Of course you are." Logan grimaced. "I just don't care to admit it."

"In the morning, we'll take her to the airport and make a plan—the three of us."

He gave Roman a brusque nod. Feeling fucking helpless was the worst. There was nothing he could do about Ava's boss. Nothing he could do to keep her from leaving. Nothing he could say to assuage her fears.

She had a life before Little Greenfield. The past eight days had existed inside a bubble. It wasn't reality. Well, it wasn't Ava's reality. Once she was home, would she forget about them? Would she abandon him? And Roman? Shit. He kicked the side of the couch and felt Roman flinch beside him.

Logan would make sure she returned. If he had to get on his bike, drive the five hours again, and carry her back kicking and screaming, he would.

She was their fucking girl.

Chapter Sixteen

AVA

Sitting in her car outside her office, Ava went over the plan they'd made before she left.

Plans were good.

She'd go into work, talk with her boss, and meet any fallout from Sebastian's vicious message head-on. Then she would confront him one last time. She had a few things at his place from when she would stay over. Nothing she'd regret losing, but it was the principle of the matter. He was the asshole, not her, so she should get her stuff back. He didn't deserve one reminder of their time together. Not a toothbrush, not a comb, not one bobby pin. Once that was done, she would call Roman and Logan and figure out what the next step in her life was. Her heart was leading her more and more to Little Greenfield.

The guys were uneasy about her confronting Sebastian without them. They feared retribution from him directed toward Ava for taking off, but she assured them she could handle it. This was something she needed to do on her own. Resist him once and for all. Make it absolutely clear that he was no longer allowed to be in her life.

At least that's what she kept telling herself.

One problem at a time.

She walked into her building, traveled to the tenth floor, and went straight down the long hallway to her boss' office. No point in putting off the inevitable. People were definitely staring at her. She would bet her left arm their whispering was about her.

Ava knocked on the mahogany door and waited for the usual *enter* to sound from behind it. When she heard her boss' voice, she opened the door and stepped inside.

Mr. Carter, who was not only her boss but the company's vice president, sat behind a sleek glass desk, a view of the Ottawa River flanked by trees turning red and gold behind him. Everything in the room was clean and meticulously organized, not a pen out of place. So the large manila folder with multi-coloured tabs sticking out haphazardly on his desk instantly drew her attention. Sign number one that something wasn't right. Shit. But maybe she was reading into things.

"Ms. Anderson, thank you for coming in on such

short notice." He gestured to the chair on the opposite side of his desk. "Please have a seat."

Ms. Anderson. Not Ava. Sign number two. A cavernous pit opened in her stomach.

She sat wordlessly, waiting for him to continue. Nothing she said was going to change whatever was about to happen, so she thought it'd be better not to stick her foot in her mouth if it could be avoided.

"Here at Method Marketing, we take the opinions of our staff seriously. We want everyone in our work environment to feel safe and comfortable."

Okay. Sign number three. Shit.

Ava chewed the inside of her cheek as she waited for the other shoe to drop. She wanted to get up, walk around, do anything other than sit with her hands folded in her lap. But that would be unprofessional, and she hoped against all odds that she was reading the signs wrong. She nodded as he continued with his obviously rehearsed speech, the words flowing through one ear and out the other before she could fully process them.

"—all that to say, Ms. Anderson, we're letting you go."

Even though everything pointed to this happening, she was still shocked. "You're…letting me go?"

"This is a reputable company. We have many clients with family owned and operated businesses. Not to mention our federal government contracts. It's on my head to make sure we are represented by people who reflect our values. I'm sure you can understand."

"And you don't think I represent the company's values? Since when?"

"Ms. Anderson, I think you are well aware of the answer to that question."

"If you're firing me, I deserve to hear you say exactly why I'm being dismissed."

Mr. Carter's eyebrows pinched together, and he straightened his tie. "Many of your colleagues heard the message that your partner sent about you. And not solely them, but myself, as well as seven high-ranking clients." Shifting in his seat, he cleared his throat. "How am I aware of this? Because those seven clients either called me or came to see me in person to voice their concerns and complaints."

"But you have to know I had nothing to do with that message. I—"

He held out a finger to silence her. "I do. I can't imagine you condoned such a thing. But you let your partner have access to your phone, which contains sensitive client information. Their data was breached on your watch. And the morality clause you signed in your contract outlined appropriate behavioural expectations. That voice message has left your reputation irrevocably tarnished, and I can't have a project manager that clients—and colleagues—don't trust."

Ava was speechless. Her gaze unfocused, eyes glossing over. Years of hard work and dedication to this place meant nothing. Now, she was a liability. There would be no convincing him otherwise.

"You will clean out your office immediately. Human Resources is waiting outside to escort you and finish the exit paperwork for your dismissal."

Any fight she had left drained out of her. She opened the door to find Marissa waiting for her. Ava allowed her to usher her to the office she'd occupied the past ten years.

How was she supposed to pack a decade's worth of shit in her office into two boxes? How was she supposed to start again somewhere else? The time she'd put in building relationships, making connections, working her way up the ladder here—none of it mattered anymore. Her chest squeezed as she gulped down a big breath of air, trying to quell her rising panic.

She hastily grabbed the most important things: binders of previously completed project outlines to add to her portfolio, and the Hoya plant she'd named Lenny. She shoved other odds and ends, like her coffee mugs and lumbar pillow, in the boxes as well. Small things were leftover. Her pencils and pens, binder clips, and folders she'd purchased to replace the generic company supplies. She didn't need it. What did it matter? It's not like she'd have a marketing job to go to after this, or any clients.

As Marissa walked her to the elevators, co-workers peeked their heads out of cubicles and offices to watch her go. All because of Sebastian. Because she had the confidence to dare ask for what she wanted in the bedroom. Because her sexual desires were supposedly a deviation from the norm.

She should've had a password on her phone, but Sebastian convinced her to remove it a few months after they started dating. It made sense at the time. *It showed trust*, he said. That *she had nothing to hide*. What a load of bullshit.

She wanted to hold her head high as she left, but her stomach was in knots and her legs were heavy—as if she were underwater. The ding of the elevator's arrival was muffled. Marissa's quick *goodbye* was deadened by the ringing in her ears.

The drive home didn't register in her brain. Somehow, she arrived outside her apartment. Like highway hypnosis, except in the city. How long had she been sitting in the underground parking? How would she afford her parking spot now that she didn't have a job? Or the rent on her place?

She took the elevator to the eighth floor and emerged, precariously balancing the boxes containing her belongings. The last thing she needed to do was drop Lenny and spill his dirt on the hallway carpet.

Stabilizing the boxes against her hip, she dug for her apartment keys in her pocket. Fucking Sebastian. This was his fault. If she'd only had the courage to dump him sooner. She needed to talk with Roman and Logan. Hear their—

What the hell? Why was *he* here? Her whole body shuddered at the sight. Who told him she was back? "Sebastian?"

"Hey, babe. I've been waiting for you."

"What are you doing here? Who let you in?"

Presenting a silver key in his hand, his eyes narrowed at her like the answer should be obvious. "I had an extra key made a long time ago. In case you ever did anything rash like taking my original copy back."

Her pulse quickened. She made a mental note to have her locks changed and talk to the security guard. "You need to leave."

He shook his head. "Now, now, Ava. You don't mean that." Sebastian leaned against her apartment door, a smarmy smirk etched on his face.

She couldn't unlock it and get inside unless he moved. After the hell of being fired from her job, the absolute last thing on Earth she wanted to deal with was him. She was supposed to do this on her terms, not be ambushed by the shithead. But he never did understand boundaries.

"I don't want to have to ask you again, Sebastian. Leave."

He clicked his tongue at her as if she were a child caught misbehaving. "You're being irrational. Why would I leave? Judging by the boxes in your arms, you were just fired, so what kind of boyfriend would I be if I left you alone?"

"Boyfriend?" Ava couldn't keep the incredulous tone out of her voice. "I dumped you last week. You are not my boyfriend."

Sebastian straightened. "We both know you didn't mean that. You were being overly sensitive, as usual. This is how you get when things don't go your way."

This behaviour was at the top of the long list of relationship cons she'd written in Little Greenfield. Gaslighting. "I meant it. You and me? We're done. Get out of my doorway."

Ava set the boxes down in front of her, creating something of a barrier between them. They were separated by a good ten feet, but it gave her the illusion of being a bit safer. Not that he'd ever laid a hand on her. He didn't have to. Sebastian fought with words, not fists.

"Ava." He took a step toward her, and she held her ground. "Who is ever going to love you, if not me? I forgive you for the breakdown you had before you took off to God-knows-where. No one else would be so kind as to overlook that. But I'm willing."

Her skin crawled at the saccharine tone he used while trying to manipulate her. It didn't match his words. Another con. "Sebastian, I need you to leave." If she kept repeating the request, he would have to listen eventually—right?

"Don't be so immature. We're going to work through this. Remember how good we were at the beginning, babe? We'll get back to that. You have to stop with your silly delusions, and be the Ava you were when we met."

"I've always been this way."

"Stop being so dense." A harsh edge creeped into his voice. "You know you've changed. What happened to my agreeable Ava?"

"You mean obedient." Her tone was flat.

"Those are your words, not mine." Another step toward her. "Everyone agrees with me. You've got a screw loose." He tapped his temple. "But I know you can work on it. I'm here to help you find your way back to normal."

"You need to leave." The urge to take a step back, to physically distance herself further from him, was overwhelming. But she didn't want to give him the satisfaction of knowing he was getting to her. She was normal, wasn't she? Roman and Logan took no issue with indulging her sexual appetite.

His nostrils flared as he stared her down. He didn't expect her rejection. "Babe, you gotta stop repeating yourself. What's wrong with you? I'm here to fix you, give you a second chance. Why are you being such a bitch?"

The word slapped her across the face. The same way it would if he used his hand. Raw, burning.

"If I don't take you back, who do you think will

want you? Huh? Nobody." Another step closer. "Men aren't tripping over themselves to be with stupid sluts like you. Get that through your thick skull."

"You're wrong," she choked out. Blinking away tears, she fought the urge to cry. She didn't want Sebastian to see how he continued to affect her, how his words stung in all her most vulnerable places. His lack of empathy was staggering.

"I'm the best you'll ever have, *babe*." He spit out the last word in disgust. "After I told everyone about your degenerate desires, no one wants to be around you, let alone be with you."

"You're wrong," she said again, trying to force a modicum of power behind her ever-shrinking voice. "I've found another man. Two, actually. They're both caring and thoughtful. And they treat me properly, like good men should treat a woman."

His laugh was brutal and harsh. "Two? You ran away and whored yourself out to two guys?" He shook his head slowly, a malicious grin eating up his face. "Well, I had you pegged, didn't I? A weak-minded little skank," he sneered.

Her shoulders slumped. She was never going to get through to him. He always had to be right. In control. Superior. Con, con, and another con. "Call me whatever you want, Sebastian. I just want you to leave. I'm done."

He strode up to her, stopping directly on the other side of her boxes. "If anyone is done, babe, it's me.

After your co-worker Nick told me you got fired, I thought I'd do the benevolent thing and take you back. But I'm not into dirty slags who throw themselves at any man who'll have them. Sorry, *men* who'll have them." He slammed his palm into the wall beside them to punctuate his point.

She couldn't help but flinch.

"Good luck, Ava. When you're two so-called *caring and thoughtful* men are done having their way with you, you'll be completely used up. Even filthier than you are now. No one will want you then."

Ava's head hung in defeat. Sebastian always had a way of tearing her down so perfectly. Always cutting her where it hurt most. Usually, he was the one to rebuild her again—how he saw fit. But not this time. This was the last time she ever wanted to see him.

She mustered the strength to say one last word. "Leave."

"You did this to yourself, Ava. Remember that." He strutted down the hall toward the stairwell.

In the past, she would've gone after him. Would've thought she made a mistake and had to fix it. That she was the one who needed to make amends.

Now, as he swaggered down the hallway in his thousand-dollar suit, most likely headed to his job at daddy's hedge fund, she didn't feel the need to call out. To go after him. To fix things. All she felt was shame. He disappeared through the stairwell door.

But he'd be back.

He always came back.

It didn't matter that he'd said he was done with her. This was how it went. She tried to defend herself. He turned it around on her. She crawled back to him. He forgave her, and the cycle continued on repeat.

Ava desperately wanted to break the cycle. Things were different. Roman and Logan were in her life now. They'd been open and accepting of what she wanted. More than that. They'd actively given her what she desired without hesitation. It had only been nine days, but they were both more supportive and considerate than Sebastian had ever been.

But when he returned, she didn't know if she would have the emotional strength to fend him off. A few minutes in the hallway with him and she shrunk like a coward. How did he always manage to do that to her? The confidence she'd built in Little Greenfield had been artfully cut down.

Tears streamed down her face as she unlocked her front door, then carried in her belongings and threw them on her dining room table. She kicked off her shoes and collapsed on her couch.

Maybe thinking she could have a life with two men *was* foolish. It wasn't the traditional way of doing things. She'd bet anything Sebastian was telling everyone she had a nervous breakdown to explain why she ran off. Can't have anyone thinking she left because he was a massive dickhole who verbally abused her on the regular.

Now that she was home in Ottawa and away from Roman and Logan, they seemed like a dream. The best damn dream she'd ever had, but still a dream.

Was it possible to begin again and move to Little Greenfield? Could she spend her life with Roman and Logan? Or rather, did they want to spend their lives with her? After knowing each other for such a short time, it was wild to think so. But her heart told her being with them was an avenue she could take, if she was brave enough to ask them what they wanted.

And if she was brave enough to convince Sebastian to leave her alone for good. Something she didn't know if she could do.

Chapter Seventeen

LOGAN

Logan paced on the front porch in the moonlight. The crickets chirping in the woods around the B&B grated on his nerves. Roman was late getting home from work. He had half a mind to call Ava himself, but Roman made him promise they'd do it together—he wanted to hear directly from Ava how things went with her boss at the same time Logan did. Under any other circumstances, Logan would probably call Roman whipped, make a joke about how needy he was, and then call Ava on his own.

But when they drove her to the airport this morning, she hadn't been herself. She was quiet, constantly shifting in her seat, and clutching her purse to her chest. Previously, her energy had been so carefree and open. To see her clam up and shut down was like seeing a different person.

Fucking hell, it made his heart sink into his stomach. A nagging in the back of his mind wouldn't leave him alone. She was bothered by more than just work. The way she'd clung to him when she realized she had to go home. How she told him it was their last night together.

The rumble of Roman's pickup echoed down the winding driveway. Fucking finally. If phones still had cords, he'd wrap it around Roman's neck for making him wait this long to check in on Ava.

"I know, I know," Roman said, making his way to stand beside Logan. "Jamie couldn't make his shift, and it got busy right before I was supposed to get off. I had to stay and close up."

Could he make his face look less impressed? He didn't think so. "It's almost midnight. She'll be sleeping."

"Did you text her and let her know we'd be calling?"

Logan cocked an eyebrow. "Of course I did."

"Then she'll be waiting up."

He balled his hands into fists. "She never replied. I've texted her"—he retrieved his phone and went through the unread messages he'd sent to Ava this evening—"sixteen times. All of them read with no reply. Something's going on."

Roman rubbed his throat. "All the more reason to

call. Right now. Let's go." He ushered Logan inside, and they sat on the bench in the foyer.

He put his phone on speaker, and they waited for Ava to pick up. And waited. And waited. And waited. He mashed the call end button and re-dialed. No answer.

"Shit!" he yelled, jumping to his feet. "There's something wrong. I can feel it."

"Take a breath, buddy. We don't know that."

Logan plunged his fingers into his hair. "But this isn't like her."

Roman stood and placed a hand on his best friend's shoulder. "It's late, and she's had a long and most likely stressful day. She's probably asleep with her phone on silent. There's a reasonable explanation."

Logan scowled at him. "Do you really believe that?"

Gathering his hair into a bun, Roman sighed. "No. You're right to worry."

"Thank you. Now, what are we going to do?"

"We're going to call one more time. If she doesn't pick up, we have to wait until morning."

Sometimes Roman's sensibility really pissed him off. But there were reasons they were best friends, and this was one of them. Roman was the calm, cool, collected match to his quick-to-anger, fire-filled soul. "One more time.."

Roman nodded his approval, and Logan dialed Ava on speakerphone again.

"Hello?" Ava's voice was drowsy on the other end of the call.

"Oh thank fuck you're alive, sweetheart," Logan practically bellowed into the phone.

"What's going on, love? We haven't heard from you all day."

"I'm really sorry. The whole day was rough. So rough and—" her voice caught and he could tell she was trying not to cry.

Logan knew it. "We're listening. If you feel ready, you can tell us everything."

"I know I was supposed to call but…I got fired. Yup. Mr. Carter had me return to let me go face-to-face. Said I wasn't family-friendly enough for the clients. I need to find a new job as soon as I can."

Logan didn't miss the way her voice cracked as she rushed through the words.

"Motherfucker. Not *family-friendly* enough? Because you're a woman that enjoys sex? I'll come down there and shove my—"

"What Logan means to say"—Roman interrupted—"is he's really sorry that happened. We both are. It's completely unfair and your personal life shouldn't have impacted your work life like that." He flashed wide eyes at Logan, wordlessly telling him to take it down a notch. "When did this happen?"

"Just before noon today."

Logan had to ask. The way she'd ignored him was driving him out of his mind. "Ava, I've texted you almost twenty times since then. You haven't responded to a single one. Is this all because you lost your job?"

Silence.

"Love, you can tell us what's happening," Roman reassured her. "Logan is tearing his hair out. And to be honest, I'm worried too. This isn't like you."

"Maybe you don't know me as well as you think." She sounded unconvinced.

"How can you say that?" Roman's eyebrows knitted together in worry as he stared at Logan.

Sniffling. Quiet sniffling. Which meant she was crying, and didn't want them to hear.

"Sebastian was right. No one is going to want me when you're done with me." Ava wept, and Logan swore a crack formed in his heart. "I'll be used and alone."

Roman jumped in immediately. "Ava, that's not true—".

"Sebastian?" Logan interrupted, irate at the mention of the dickhole's name. "This is because of fucking Sebastian? When did you talk to him? What did he do?"

"He was waiting for me at my apartment. I thought I could be free. When I met you both, it seemed like I could finally be me and be happy. But he'll come back for me. He always does."

He couldn't take it anymore. This. Fucking. Guy. He shoved his phone into Roman's hands and stormed out the front door into the cool night air.

Roman would say the right things.

Roman would calm Ava down and make her see reason.

There was no point in him yelling through the phone at Ava. It wasn't her he was mad at. He was livid with her no good, asswipe, son-of-a-bitch ex-boyfriend. Ex being the keyword. And he was going to stay that way.

How dare he tell her she would be used and alone. That no one would want her. This guy had *narcissist* written all over him. After listening to the little one-man show he put on for Ava's contacts, he'd suspected as much. No one in their right mind would do that to someone they loved. Sebastian wasn't capable of love. He lived to manipulate, which he was still doing to Ava.

Showing up at her home uninvited.

Putting her down.

Making her believe she was worthless.

When Roman got off the phone, he would call Jerry and make him fly them to Ottawa tomorrow. He didn't care that it was after midnight. He'd promise Jerry a year's worth of free drinks at The White Pine Pub. Flight plans were probably a thing that needed to happen, but he had no clue about that. He was supposed to fly Ava home tomorrow, anyway. If anyone could make it work, Jerry would.

Because he was going to see Ava as soon as possible.

And he was going to fucking kill Sebastian.

ROMAN

"Come back, Ava. We'll take care of you."

"I don't know if I can. "

He gripped the phone tightly, wishing it was Ava he was holding on to. "You don't mean that, love. You don't."

"Thank you. For the time I got to spend with you. For treating me so well. Tell Logan I say thank you, too."

"Ava. This is bullshit. I'm sorry if that sounds harsh, but it's true. This isn't the Ava I know."

She was quiet on the other end, but her steady breaths sounded through the line.

"You're coming back to us. End of story."

"I told you Sebastian was done with me, but he says that all the time. He won't actually let me go, and I want to be strong enough to tell him off, but I don't know if I am."

"Fucking tough. He can come to Little Greenfield and try to get you back. We'll tell him no for you."

More silence. More tears he wished he could reach through the phone and wipe away.

"This is what you want? Both of you?" Hope filled her voice.

His insides ached at the question. "Of course it is, love. Do you really doubt?"

"Sebastian really got in my head. Everything's been so fast with you and Logan. I want to make sure this is what you both want, too."

"Ava, we'll be there tomorrow. So gather your things. Everything you want to have for the next few weeks, pack. We'll worry about the rest later."

He prayed to the universe that she was nodding in the silence on the other end of the line.

"Do you hear me, love? I need you to answer me."

"I hear you." Her voice was more confident now.

"Good. We'll be there as soon as we can. Go to sleep and don't give that jag another second of your thoughts. Dream of me. I'll be dreaming of you."

"Goodnight, Roman."

"Goodnight, love."

The flirty, wonderful woman he'd fallen for was shaken. All in less than a day. He understood some people were capable of holding a kind of power over others, but he'd never witnessed it until now.

The way Ava talked about herself tonight was proof that Sebastian had been manipulating and controlling her for a long period of time.

If he ever saw Sebastian, he'd lay him out flat on

his egotistical ass. Logan would be itching to put him in his place as well. It wouldn't surprise him if he was planning how to hurt the motherfucker in the worst possible way.

But Ava was his before she was Logan's. If anyone—and he meant anyone—said that she was used up or deserved to be alone, he would work them till they were bloody and broken.

No one talked about their girl that way. No one.

They got a later start than Roman wanted. He texted Ava to let her know. Jerry was stuck waiting for flight plan approval since he'd cancelled Ava's original return. The all clear didn't come until the early afternoon. They were lucky to get out considering how last minute it was. Again. Still, he would've driven the five hours to the city in his pickup if that's what was necessary.

A taxi met them at Ottawa's Rockcliffe Airport—an old military base where Jerry was a member of the flying club—and drove them downtown to The Carlisle, the high-rise apartment building where Ava lived.

Ava buzzed them in, and Logan whistled in appreciation at the lobby. Roman couldn't blame him. The walls were full paneled wainscotting with black marble accent tiles. A modern chandelier hung from the recessed and backlit ceiling. Plush silver armchairs dotted the front windows, creating cozy conversation areas.

"Not the place I pictured her living," Logan said, striding swiftly toward the elevators.

Roman kept pace beside him. "I didn't picture her anywhere. She was just part of our life at the bed and breakfast. Seemed at home there."

Logan jabbed the up button. "Well, if her job allowed her to live here, I can understand her being in a rush to find another one."

The elevator arrived, and they stepped inside. Roman hit the button for the eighth floor and drummed his fingers against his side. The defeat in Ava's voice from last night plagued his thoughts. She sounded so unlike the woman who stumbled into his pub nine days ago. He couldn't help but worry about her.

"Hey," Logan said, swatting his shoulder. "Get out of your head. We're bringing her home with us. Even if I have to throw her over my shoulder again."

Roman frowned. "Again?"

Logan smirked as the elevator chimed and opened.

Roman stalked down the hall, searching for apartment 809. He found it halfway down, and it took all his willpower to knock on the door instead of kicking it down and running inside to Ava.

"Ava," he called. "It's us. Open up, please, love. We need to see you."

A second later, she answered the door. Her hair was in a messy bun on top of her head, curls spilling out every which way. Mascara stained her cheeks. Her baggy t-shirt and pink sweats did nothing to hide her slumped posture. She looked like a woman defeated. In no way would he stand for that.

He gathered her into his arms and held her close, relieved to have her in his embrace after such a shit night. She wrapped her arms around his waist and buried her face against his chest.

After a long moment, Logan cleared his throat. "You're occupying the whole doorway, Roman."

He murmured an apology and side-stepped around Ava, walking into her home, while Logan greeted her with a kiss on her forehead.

The apartment had walnut cabinets, similar in colour to the hardwood floors. White granite accents and cream-coloured walls rounded out the space. Cozy, warm. Very much like Ava.

Fuzzy blankets and fluffy pillows of various shapes and sizes covered a taupe sectional. Succulents dotted the kitchen and living room, a few hung from the ceiling. Bookshelves flanked the floor-to-ceiling windows showcasing the other downtown high-rise buildings. She fit in this space well, but the B&B seemed more like her home.

Logan scanned the entryway. "Where are your bags, Ava?"

"Isn't this a little quick?" she asked, leaning into Logan's side.

Roman shrugged. "Sure it is. But that doesn't mean it's not the correct choice."

"He's right. Show me where your bags are so I can get them for you. Then we're taking you home."

"What about my apartment? Finding another job?" The worry crept back into her voice.

Roman held out his hand to her, and she left Logan to accept it. "It can all wait. Your apartment will still be here. As for your job, consider this a sabbatical. We'll figure out the rent for this place."

She nodded against his chest. "Okay. One step at a time."

"Bags, Ava," Roman urged.

"In there." She pointed to a door off the living room.

Logan disappeared through it. Rustling noises were followed by him emerging with two bags in his hands and one across his shoulder. "Let's go."

"You're sure you have everything, love?"

"I went through my bags four times while waiting for you. I double checked the apartment—everything's turned off or unplugged." She inhaled a deep breath as if to steady herself. "I'm ready."

Roman took her hand and led them out of her apartment.

She locked the door behind her and tucked the keys inside her purse. "Sebastian has a key to my place. I was going to change the locks."

"Is there anything left in the apartment that you don't want him to get his hands on?"

She shook her head. "Everything important is packed in those bags."

Roman ran his thumb in circles on the back of her hand. "Then we'll add the locks to our to-do list. But it's not something we need to concern ourselves with right now."

"And what about my car? I didn't think about that."

"Your building has parking?" Logan asked.

"Yeah. Heated and underground."

"Then it's fine. As soon as you want it in Little Greenfield, Roman and I will drive here and get it for you."

Ava's mouth fell open slightly, and she stared at Logan. "You would, wouldn't you?"

Both he and Logan nodded their agreement.

A new resolve seemed to fill her. She stood with her shoulders back and raised her chin.

There she was. A glimpse of his Ava.

"Okay, then. Let's do this." Her hold on him tightened.

They descended in the elevator to the lobby, Logan standing protectively in front. A smile tugged the corner of Ava's lips. Roman's heart fluttered at the sight of her spirit returning, even in small amounts.

"I bet Jerry wasn't too pleased about having to fly to Ottawa again today," Ava mused, glancing at Roman as they stepped into the lobby.

"Once I offered him free drinks at the pub for the next month—"

"Year," Logan corrected.

Roman laughed. "Year," he continued, "he was more than willing to fly us out here."

Ava squeezed his hand and smiled at him. A bright, beautiful smile. He could stare at that smile and never want for anything more.

And then it vanished.

In its place, fear.

Roman followed Ava's gaze to a tall man heading toward them. The stranger's nostrils were flared, and his fingers kept flexing, but his face was a picture of calm. He wore a fancy navy suit, cut perfectly to fit, and his eyes were trained on Ava

There was no doubt in Roman's mind. This was Sebastian.

He stopped a few feet from them, clearly sizing them up. "What's going on, babe?" Sebastian's stare jumped from her, to Roman, to Logan.

Ava didn't answer.

She huddled against Roman, her eyes downcast. Stepping to her other side, Logan set down her bags and placed his palm in hers.

If Sebastian was at all intimidated, he didn't show it.

"Babe, I'm here to apologize. Let's go up to your place so we can talk."

"We have nothing to talk about." Ava's voice sounded timid.

"Of course we do." Sebastian stepped toward her and Roman instinctively closed in at the same time as Logan did, presenting a united front. "You're my one and only, Ava. We need to work through this…little hiccup." He gestured to the men at her sides.

Her sigh was heavy. "You said you were done with me, Sebastian."

"I didn't mean it, babe, you know that. You upset me, remember? How else was I supposed to react to you running away and living with two strangers?"

She shook her head. "Not like that."

"So let me take you upstairs, and we can talk. One-on-one. I'm the only real, honest person left in your life, Ava. You don't want to turn your back on that, do you?"

"I think that's enough," Roman said, stern but calm, keeping the rising anger out of his voice.

Ava's ex was a bigger jerk than she let on. Sebastian's attempt to manipulate her was painfully obvious. Roman tucked her behind him, and Logan followed suit, removing his hand from hers and standing in front of her as well.

Sebastian glared at him, hands clenched at his

sides. "I wasn't talking to you, meathead." He peered between Roman and Logan, trying to lock eyes with Ava. "You can't be serious about these two piss-flaps, babe."

"Wanna insult us again?" Logan taunted.

"I'm warning you, babe." Sebastian still refused to meet his or Logan's gaze. "I've given you a lot of second chances. This is the last one. Come with me now, or else."

Logan's humourless laugh filled the lobby. "Or else what, fuckface? You're gonna send another bitch-boy voice message to her family and co-workers? You're gonna air her dirty laundry to her clients?"

If life was a cartoon, steam would be pouring from his best friend's ears. But it wasn't. Instead, life had pricks like Sebastian who took advantage of sweet women like Ava. He knew Logan's patience was wearing thin.

"So, this is your choice? Two losers from the middle of nowhere instead of the man who has loved you for the past two years?"

Roman let out a bitter scoff. "How you treated Ava is the furthest thing from love."

Sebastian shook his head. "I thought you were better than this, babe."

"You're right. I *am* better than this. Better than *you*, Sebastian." Ava's voice wavered, but the quiet resolve in her tone was unmistakable.

"I think it's time for you to leave before I make

you leave." Logan invaded Sebastian's personal space, daring him to make a move.

Finally, Sebastian made eye contact with Logan. A sneer spoiled his once-handsome face, contorting his features to show the true beast underneath.

"You want her? Do you even know her? What her perverted little mind thinks about?" He laughed, a cold sound that didn't meet his eyes. "Of course you know." He lowered his voice. "Does she take both your dicks at once? Do you pass her around? What a fucking slut—"

Logan pinned him against the nearest wall. The breath left Sebastian's lungs from the force of being knocked against the marble tiles. Logan's hand wrapped around his throat while his knee pressed against his groin.

Sebastian's eyes bulged.

"You don't call her that," Logan growled an inch from his face. "No one does. Except me—and strictly when I'm fucking her so good, she's screaming my name, begging for more."

A wheezing sound came from Sebastian's constricted throat. His hands desperately tried to pry off Logan's chokehold.

"That's enough," Roman said. "He's had enough."

Logan remained lost in his rage. And Sebastian's face was turning an ugly shade of purple.

"Logan—enough!" Roman yelled, his voice echoed off the walls.

Ava clutched Roman's arm. "Logan!"

At the sound of her voice, Logan released Sebastian. He sagged to the floor, doubled over, coughing and retching.

"He deserves worse." Logan's voice was low and menacing.

"I know." Ava's voice was pinched but stronger than before. "I know. Thank you for standing up for me. Both of you."

They embraced her, acting as a shield from the dickbag-of-a-human struggling to catch his breath on the floor.

"Let's go before I really lose my temper, and something worse happens." Logan grabbed Ava's bags and headed for the lobby's front door.

Roman ushered Ava ahead of him as Sebastian staggered to his feet, leaning on the wall for support.

"I hope you both enjoy my sloppy seconds and her big, stretched-out puss—"

A loud crunch filled the air as his fist collided with Sebastian's face.

Out of the corner of his eye, he saw Ava startle and grip Logan. He towered over Sebastian, who lay in a heap on the floor, holding his nose while blood poured between his fingers.

Roman flexed and shook out his hand.

"What the hell, man?" Sebastian cried. "You can't

go around sucker-punching people. My dad's lawyers will—"

Roman bent down—mere inches from his face—and Sebastian recoiled. "Real men don't run to daddy's lawyers. And real men don't treat women the way you do. Love is love. But since you're incapable of that, I don't expect you and your tiny, intolerant brain to understand."

It took everything in him to not spit his hatred on the man's pathetic face. "Never contact Ava again. Never come near her. Never speak her name. Or next time, you won't be so fucking lucky."

He spun to face Ava and Logan. "Let's go."

Logan nodded and escorted Ava out of the building. Roman followed closely behind, leaving the miserable excuse for a man bleeding on the floor.

Chapter Eighteen

AVA

The last two days were a blur. Between the flight to Ottawa, getting fired, Sebastian berating her, being rescued by Roman and Logan, and returning to Little Greenfield—she was exhausted.

She stretched out on the guest suite bed. The images of Logan choking Sebastian, followed by Roman smashing his nose, wouldn't leave her mind. She replayed them again and again.

Logan squeezing Sebastian's throat.

The crack of Roman's fist against Sebastian's face.

The way he cowered on the floor.

It gave her a sick sense of satisfaction. Was it normal to feel so satisfied watching your ex-boyfriend get what he deserved? It didn't matter. She'd never wished physical harm on him before, but seeing it play out was gratifying.

Roman and Logan cared about her. She'd have to be blind not to see that. But she didn't realize how much until they arrived on her doorstep. She didn't need a pros list any longer. Why would she? Her two men were the epitome of everything on said list.

When she saw Sebastian walking into her lobby, her heart sank. She thought he'd convince her to give him another chance, repeating the same cycle she always went through, though she recognized how wrong it was. How unhealthy.

But Roman and Logan didn't let that happen. They'd protected her. They'd given her the confidence to tell him off.

She'd spent two long years with Sebastian. Not once did she ever feel loved by him the way she felt loved by Roman and Logan. Could she use that word —love—already? Probably not. She shouldn't jump to words like that after being in a dysfunctional relationship with Sebastian for so long. How many times had she said *I love you* to him? Too many to count.

But it wasn't genuine love. The kind that made a person feel safe and secure. The kind a person saw in movies and read about in Jane Austen novels. The kind that made a person's toes curl and heart beat faster.

Sebastian's love was toxic. Rotten. Defective. But after he'd told her so many times that no one else would love her, and how he was the one person who could take care of her, she started to believe it. Repeat something enough times and it feels like reality.

She got up, checked the clock beside the bed, and saw the time was almost eleven in the morning. Draping a throw blanket around her shoulders, she opened the glass doors to the balcony and went outside. The cool breeze caressed her face, and she shivered, savouring the moment.

So did she love Roman? Logan? She didn't know.

Love was hard.

Love was complicated.

But it was also fierce, free, and all-consuming.

"You're awake," Roman called to her from below.

She peered over the railing. Roman stood below, looking like the manliest man she'd ever seen. Hair tied up in a bun, plaid fleece tight around his biceps. Work gloves stretched across his thick fingers, and dark jeans hugged his ass. He was loading a pile of split logs into the wagon beside him.

Ava smiled down at him.

"I thought you might sleep the entire day with how quickly you were out last night."

"I'm drained, but I should probably get ready for the day. I can't remember the last time I slept past ten."

His chuckle filled her with delight. The deep, throaty sound had quickly become one of her favourites.

"Can I bring you breakfast in bed? Logan fixed you a plate this morning, but didn't want to wake you."

"I'll come down. Thank you, though."

"Anything for you. You know that." He winked at her and started stripping off his gloves.

She quickly brushed her teeth, threw her hair into a ponytail, and dressed in her favourite low-cut sweater and a pair of black boy-shorts. It was the weird time of year where the temperature was cold one second, and hot the next. Almost like Mother Nature was trying to hold on to the last remnant of summer, but didn't quite have the strength left to fight off the autumn chill.

She shuffled down the stairs, wiping the exhaustion from her eyes. Roman was waiting for her in the kitchen with a plate of fruit, a yogurt parfait, a croissant, and a mug of tea. He'd set it all out at the breakfast bar and pulled out a stool for her.

Her stomach rumbled and her mouth watered at the delicious looking spread. "Thank you. This looks amazing."

"You should thank Logan, but since he's not here, I'll graciously accept."

She took a bite of the croissant and put her palm on her heart. "I will definitely be thanking Logan when he gets home."

Roman rounded the counter to stand next to her. "I want to apologize."

"For Logan not being here?" she asked around a mouthful of flaky pastry.

"For hitting Sebastian. I shouldn't have done that." He took her hands in his. "Attacking him was wrong, and I take full responsibility for letting my anger get the best of me."

Ava swallowed what was the best bite of a croissant she'd ever had and tried her best to suppress her smile. Roman was being serious, so she had to be too.

"You don't have to apologize. If we're being honest, Sebastian deserved it. I'd like to say it'll be a wake-up call for him, but he's too much of a narcissist."

Roman's shoulders relaxed. "I was so worried you were upset."

Her gaze softened. "At you? Are you kidding?"

Roman shook his head.

This time, she couldn't help but laugh. "Roman, I've no reason to be mad at you. You came for me. You removed me from a terrible situation. You defended my honour like a medieval knight." She slipped her hands out of his and grabbed his face, lowering it to hers. "I'm not upset. I'm thankful. So, so thankful."

She kissed him, and he opened eagerly for her. He separated her legs, settling close against her body, and she forgot all about breakfast. Their mouths slanted against each other, and his tongue swept deep inside her mouth, possessive and devouring.

His tattooed fingers ran up her thighs and tucked underneath her ass. He squeezed before lifting her to him, and she wrapped her legs around his waist. Carrying her to the couch, he ran his lips and teeth down her neck, nipping and biting. She rubbed against him, aching for more. His tongue licked down her chest and he buried his face between her breasts.

Roman kneeled and placed her softly on the couch, remaining between her legs. His fingers hooked in the waistband of her shorts and tugged gently.

"I want nothing more than to rip these off you so I can give you the best fucking head of your life. But if it's too soon, and you need time, just say the word and I'll stop." His tone was desperate, yet controlled.

She had no doubt he would stop immediately if she gave the word. But that wasn't what she wanted. "I need you, Roman. I need you now." She lifted her hips, and he yanked her shorts and underwear down and threw them across the room.

"Take this off," he demanded, tugging at the hem of her sweater.

She quickly lifted it overhead and tossed it somewhere behind her.

He licked his lips at the sight of her. "God fucking dammit, Ava. Are you trying to kill me?"

There was no point in playing coy. Not putting on a bra today was a purposeful choice.

Roman palmed her breasts, sucking one of her

nipples into his mouth, then the other. His thick fingers skimmed her inner thigh. A gasp escaped her as he cupped her forcefully, rubbing the heel of his palm against her clit.

"I've missed this pussy so much," he groaned.

"Show me."

Roman pushed one finger inside her, twisting and pressing deep. Her head fell back against the couch, and she closed her eyes. His finger slipped out and was joined by another, pressing into her harder this time. She whimpered at the intrusion, breath picking up, squirming against his hand.

He dipped down, dragging his tongue over her cunt slowly, teasing her with every lick. "You taste so fucking good, love."

"More, Roman. I need more," she whined, aching to feel the scratch of his beard on her thighs. To have more of him inside her.

"Use me, Ava. Ride my fingers," he grunted against her pussy, shoving a third inside her. He pumped them in a heated rhythm. "Ride my face." Using his free hand on the small of her back, he pushed her against him. "Ride me," he growled.

Ava's hands found the back of his head, and she shoved him tight against her pussy. Clamping her thighs around him, she bucked her hips against his mouth, his fingers pressing deeper still. She lost herself in the motion, in the way he sucked on her clit, in the fullness of the fingers inside her.

Heat spread from her belly to her limbs. Roman's tongue moved fervently against her as she chased her orgasm, fucking herself on his face. Using him for what she needed. Her legs shook against his head.

She was so close. So close.

"Dirty girl." Logan's dangerously low voice filled the room. The front door slammed behind him.

Roman didn't miss a beat and continued sucking at her, spearing her with his three thick digits, forcing her against his face with his hand on her back.

She opened her eyes and met Logan's gaze. He looked like he wanted to wrap his fingers around her throat and choke her with his dick. The intensity made her pussy clench around Roman's fingers.

"Come for him, Ava. Come on his face. I want to see you drown him in your release." His voice was dark and animalistic. "Then, it's my turn."

Logan undid his pants, shoved down the front of his underwear, and freed his hard cock. Her orgasm crashed through her. Heat flooded her body, and she held tight to Roman's hair. He lapped at her arousal, licking it off her thighs, shoving his tongue in her pussy to taste more. She collapsed against the couch, and her thighs fell from Roman's head.

He kissed his way up her body and licked into her mouth. His face was slick with her cum, but she didn't care. She welcomed the warmth of his mouth on hers.

"So good, love. Your pussy is so fucking perfect."

He bit down on her neck, causing her to buck once more beneath him. “I need to have you. Tell me I can fuck you. I’m dying here, Ava,” he breathed against her collarbone.

“I don’t think it’s up to me.”

When he leaned back, she pointed behind him, and he turned to see Logan standing a few feet away, cock hard and in hand.

“She’s mine now,” Logan challenged.

Roman stood and wiped his face with the back of his hand. “I got her off and you expect me to just give her to you?” He puffed out his chest as he took a step closer to Logan.

“Sharing is caring.” Logan smirked, walking around Roman to her. “On your knees, sweetheart.”

He pinched the bridge of his nose. “No fucking way, I—”

“Roman,” Ava said softly, holding her hand out to him. He joined her, and she rubbed soothing circles along his knuckles. “I’ll be with you after.”

He plowed his fingers through his hair. “Okay, but later we need to lay down some ground rules for how we do…this.” He gestured to Logan and Ava, then himself.

Logan nodded. “Fine.”

“I promise we’ll do that,” she agreed. “Can you stay and watch?”

Roman cursed, his eyes lighting up. “Would you like that?”

Without taking her gaze off of Roman's face, she dropped to her knees in front of Logan and nodded.

"Then I'll watch, love." Roman went to the overstuffed easy chair and sat down. His gaze was glued to her. He lifted his chin in Logan's direction, coaxing her on.

Logan placed his hand on her cheek. "Suck."

She leaned in and grabbed his thighs while she ran her tongue up the length of his shaft. When she got to the tip, she sucked it into her mouth and swirled her tongue around it.

He gave her ponytail a warning tug. "I said suck, Ava."

She was coming to understand that Logan was incredibly dominant in sex, and liked to get his way. But when she circled him with her tongue, his thigh muscles tensed beneath her hands. He enjoyed her teasing touch, even if he wouldn't admit it.

She gripped the base of his cock with one palm and took him deep into her mouth, nearly swallowing him whole. The stretch of her lips was the right amount of uncomfortable, and she moaned at the feel of him inside her.

He tasted like sin.

On the other side of the room, Roman's voice rumbled his encouragement. "You're so fucking hot with his cock in your mouth, love."

She timed her hand to be in tandem with her mouth, traveling up and down Logan's length, his spray of pubic hair brushing her nose with each movement. She went a little lower each time until she felt him touch the back of her throat. She gagged and let her saliva pool around him as she worked.

"Fuck," Logan hissed between clenched teeth. "Oh fuck. Yes, Ava. Yes."

She quickened her pace. The vocalization of his pleasure was like a drug. Never had she enjoyed giving head to a man as much as she did to Logan. She brought him deep, pulled back to his tip, then took him deep again while twisting her hand alongside her mouth. Choking on him was a pleasure all on its own.

"Should I fuck her face, Roman? Make her take me how I need?"

When Roman groaned his agreement, Ava's heart skipped a beat.

"You're going to be a good girl and take it, yes?"

She nodded her approval, hungry for the feel of his power, and let him take control.

He grabbed her ponytail close to the roots. Dropping her hand, she relaxed her jaw and throat and let him have his way with her.

"Fuck, Ava. Such a dirty girl for me. Gag on my cock like the perfect slut you are."

Logan set a punishing pace, bucking into her mouth. The grip on her hair tightened. Saliva dripped off her chin, and she suffocated on his cock, loving that he trusted her with his brutality. Her pulse increased, and the wetness between her legs became uncomfortable. She ached for him. For Roman. For them both.

"I'm going to come," Logan panted. "And as much as I want you to swallow, I want to see your tits coated with my cum like the messy whore you are."

"You're doing so well, love," Roman grunted.

She moaned around Logan's dick. If she was wet before, she was saturated now.

Logan yanked her head back, and his cock slid out of her throat. She gasped, catching her breath. Hot spurts of cum decorated her chest as Logan stroked out his release.

"Such a perfect slut," he praised her, running his thumb over her bottom lip. "So pretty painted in my cum."

"Touch me, Logan. Feel me, please," she begged.

Without hesitation, he dropped to his knees alongside her and slipped his fingers between the lips of her pussy.

"Fucking hell, you're wet, Ava. My god," he moaned, lowering his mouth to her cunt.

"No." She shook her head, dragging him back up. "I need you inside me. And I need..." She eyed her tattooed man, sitting in the corner, watching her every move. "I need Roman, too."

"Ava..." Logan said slowly, eyebrows squeezing together.

"I know you're unsure about it. I know," she

soothed, placing a palm on his chest. "And I won't force you to do anything. But I want this—all three of us. Roman is good with it, but you haven't made it clear if you'd be willing to try it, too."

"Shit." He closed his eyes briefly. "Yes, Ava. I'll give it a go. Honestly, any chance I get to be with you, I'll take."

She squealed and threw her arms around Logan's neck, hugging him tight. "Oh!" She drew back, staring at his button-down shirt now stained with his cum. "Sorry about that."

Logan laughed. A sound, musical and deep, she didn't hear often, though she wished she did. "Don't worry about it. I need to clean you up, anyway."

He stripped off his shirt and used it to wipe the mess off Ava's chest.

Roman stood beside her. "Let's go." He offered his hand and helped her to her feet. "We need to do this while you're still soaked, love."

Chapter Nineteen

AVA

Logan ushered her through his doorway, insisting they use his bedroom. Sleek and modern, his room was completely different from Roman's. Not a thing out of place. Multiple lamps cast a warm glow across everything, bathing the room in amber light and shadows. She hadn't noticed any of this when she'd first been in here. Probably because she was too busy getting the brains fucked out of her head to care about the lamplight.

"Get on the bed, Ava," Logan ordered. "On your back. Legs spread wide."

She did as she was told. She always did as she was told with Logan. How he and Roman would function together in this kind of situation, she didn't know. Logan was dominant and authoritative. He claimed and controlled what he wanted. Roman was sweet, giving, and willing to do whatever she desired. His begging was a turn-on in its own right.

"Touch yourself," Logan commanded.

She slid her fingers down her stomach, still sticky from Logan's release, and closed her eyes. When she found her clit, she released a sharp gasp and treated herself tenderly. The sensation was overwhelming, but she didn't dare stop and disobey Logan.

"Oh, hell," Roman said. "You're so fucking gorgeous, love." He fell to his knees at the foot of the bed. "I could spend every waking moment kneeling before you and die a lucky man."

The warmth of his hands stroking her thighs elicited a quiet sob from her throat. She opened her eyes and saw him watching her from between her legs, his stare fixed on her fingers playing with her clit. Logan stood behind him, stripping off his pants slowly, eyes locked on her own.

Her entire being was on high alert. Being watched elevated her arousal. All eyes on her. Goosebumps pebbled her arms and legs. Her fingers rubbed frantically against pussy while her hips bucked against the empty air. She needed their touch. She craved their friction.

"Strip, Roman," Logan commanded.

Roman stood and obeyed, never taking his eyes off of her.

The sight of her two men, standing side-by-side,

naked in all their glory, was her wet dream. Logan's cut torso, the trail of hair that led to his perfectly thick cock. Roman's broad shoulders, tattooed chest, and long, pierced dick. They were too much. They were everything. The orgasm that rocked through her was sharp and biting. She let out a scream as the height of pleasure shook her from the inside out.

"I can't wait any longer." Roman climbed between her legs and slipped inside her. He met no resistance.

The intrusion was almost painful for how tender she was, but she reveled in it.

"Your pussy feels amazing, love. All I want to do is fuck you. I see you, and I want to eat you," he murmured in her ear. "I want to be inside you. I want to make you call out my name."

He rocked into her in a steady rhythm, his piercing grinding against her most sensitive spot, making her stomach clench with need.

"That's enough." Logan's voice was stern in his warning.

Roman laughed in her ear. "Like hell it is."

"Ava—do you still want both of us?"

Logan's comment made Roman go still inside her. He smiled. "You ready for us…together?"

She nodded. "I need you both."

He pulled out, leaving her empty and raw, and stood over her. The tattoos snaking around his neck, biceps, and arms looked delicious in the warm glow of the lamplight. He was a picture of power and need. She saw it in his eyes. The hunger. The thirst. The want.

Roman stroked his cock, raking his eyes down her naked form. "I want your ass."

She caught herself licking her lips and hummed her approval. "It's yours."

"I've already had it," Logan chimed in, climbing on the bed beside her, lying on his back. "You're gonna fucking love it, Banks."

"I have no doubts about that," Roman quipped.

"Get on top of me, Ava." Logan's simple demand made her cunt clench.

She needed to fill it with something, and the idea of it being Logan had her leaking down her thighs.

She climbed onto him and gripped his cock, ready to lower herself, when Logan reached out and stopped her.

"Not yet, sweetheart." He drew her close to him, so her tits were pressed against his chest and her cheek rested on his shoulder. He gently tugged the elastic out of her hair, releasing her curls. "Ass up."

The bed sunk behind her as Roman positioned himself. The cap to a bottle of lube clicked open, and the squirt sounded obscene in the dim light. His finger rubbed against her tight hole, massaging, drawing slow circles around it.

Suddenly, Roman's finger penetrated her ass, and she gasped loudly, pressing into him. She arched her back, raising her hips to give him better access. He slipped in and out easily, prepping her for what was coming.

"Was Logan your first here?" Roman asked, working his finger inside her.

"Yes," she moaned, loving the feel of him playing with this forbidden part of her.

"Did you like it?"

"So much."

"She fucking loved it," Logan said, stroking her hair. "My filthy girl came so hard she soaked my bed."

A second finger pressed into her, slippery with lube, and she hissed at the intrusion, grazing her teeth over Logan's collarbone.

"You can bite if you need to," Logan purred in her ear. "Don't be shy, Ava."

"Oh my God, Roman. I need you. Now. Please fuck me, please," she pleaded, longing for more.

He chuckled. "It's nice to hear you beg for once, love. You're almost ready."

A third finger joined the others, and she sank her teeth into Logan's shoulder.

He grunted in her ear and grabbed her hips. "That's it, sweetheart. Be rough with me."

Roman was torturing her in the most excruciating and luxurious way while Logan's whispers in her ear drove her out of her mind.

"Please, Roman. Please." A sob escaped her throat. "Please fuck me. I need more."

Logan gripped her chin and brought her face to his, kissing her so deeply she saw fireworks behind her eyelids. Roman's cock notched at her asshole, and she didn't give him time to waste. She pushed against him, desperate for the feel of him inside her.

His cock slipped inside and she exhaled, forcing herself to relax. Like she did with her toys at home. Like she did with Logan. Nothing compared to this feeling. So strange, so wrong. The vulgar nature of it made her wet. His piercing was a brand new sensation, and she welcomed the feel of the metal bar inside her, relishing the friction it gave.

A low rumble built in Roman's throat. "Shit, Logan. You were right. I do fucking love it. Her ass was made to take our cocks."

"You're goddamn right. Now fuck our girl," Logan ordered.

Roman pumped in and out, and in again. Filling her. Using her. The intrusion of his cock in her most profane place was everything she wanted.

Logan's fingers found her clit, and he played with her exactly how she liked it. Fast and firm. Gliding side to side inside her slit.

"Yes, Ava, yes. Your ass is so fucking tight around my cock." Roman's voice was thick and raw with lust.

Her orgasm crashed into her unexpectedly, and her cum flooded Logan's lap and hand, soaking the skin between them. Two sensations fought for dominance—agony and toe-curling ecstasy. She cried out into Logan's shoulder, biting down hard enough to break his skin.

"Fuck, yes, dirty girl," he growled. "Hurt me."

Roman slowed his thrusts as she caught her breath, sweat clinging to her body, hair mussed and in her face.

Logan swept a curl out of her eyes and gripped the nape of her neck. "I'm going to join him now."

All she could do was nod.

Roman held still while Logan's hand shifted from her clit to his cock, guiding it into her pussy with care. There was little resistance, considering how soaked she was. A sense of incredible fullness astounded her. Never in her life had she been so full.

"I can feel him inside you, Ava," Roman whispered as he kissed the back of her shoulder. "It's so tight."

Logan grunted his agreement. "I don't hate it."

"Admit it. You love it," Roman ribbed.

"I'm cock deep in Ava's pussy. I'd like her to fuck us now."

She loved how they could both be buried to the hilt in her and still chirp at each other like they always did. She couldn't help but grin. Lifting her head to look at Logan, she said, "I'm not doing anything until you tell Roman."

He raised his eyebrow at her, but she returned his disbelief with a challenging stare of her own.

"Fine," he grumbled. "It feels fucking fantastic. Happy?"

She nipped at his lip, enjoying having him at her mercy. "Almost. Tell Roman, not me."

Logan titled his head so he could see Roman. "It's so fucking good." He bucked his hips into her, and she groaned at the same time as Roman. "I want to fuck you both like this every night." He bucked against them again.

A yelp escaped her lips, and Roman wrapped his arms around her, clasping onto her tits and groaning into her hair.

"You think you can order me around? I'm the one in control here. Don't forget that." Logan jerked his hips into them one more time.

Her eyes rolled into the back of her head while Roman uttered a curse under his breath. "Now fuck us, my pretty little slut. Work us until you scream."

Ava rocked herself gently against them, adjusting to the two cocks inside her, slowly increasing her pace. Nothing had ever been this good. Spent and covered in sweat, pressed between her two men, she rejoiced in the moment's freedom. No one to tell her it was wrong. No one to shame her desires.

The three of them were joined in a pumping mass of passion and lust and devotion, crying out to each other in their ecstasy. Roman's power and Logan's control surrounded her. Sharing her as she shared them. Another orgasm was out of the question for her, but she didn't care. All she wanted right now was for her two men to finish inside her, to claim her as their own.

Roman was beginning to tremble behind her, and Logan's breathing was harsh and fast. They were close.

"Logan. Roman. Come for me," she cried.

Her breasts, her hips, her hair—hands grasped her, and she lost track of who was who. Roman roared out his release like the bear of a man he was. Logan hissed through his teeth, uttering a string of vulgarities in her ear.

They collapsed in a heap of heads, and hands, and hearts. Bodies intertwined and clutching each other, like they couldn't let go if they tried.

Her chest heaved with exertion. Sweat beaded in Roman's chest hair. Logan's shoulder was red and raw with her bites.

"Can we stay like this for a while?" she asked, her voice small as she relaxed between them.

Roman rubbed her hip. "Whatever you need, love."

"We're here for you, sweetheart," Logan echoed.

ROMAN

"Move to Little Greenfield," Roman said, rolling onto his side so he could look into Ava's eyes. "Be with us. Really be with us."

She held his gaze. Tenderness reflected in her stare. His heart jumped when she focused on him like that.

He couldn't imagine her saying no.

A half an hour had passed since their barrier-shattering sex, and they were still lounging in bed together, the three of them descending from their high.

"There's a lot to consider, Roman. I've never thought about leaving Ottawa before."

"What's there that's better than here?" Logan asked, reclining against the headboard, stroking his finger lazily across her bare breast. "Be specific."

"I—" Her forehead wrinkled, like she was trying her hardest to think of a suitable answer. "Actually, I don't know. I would've said my career, but that's gone now. I would've said my boyfriend, but he's history. I guess some of my friends are in the city, but I've alienated most of them. I couldn't tell you where any of them are in their lives." She groaned and buried her head in the sheets. "Am I a terrible person?"

"No," Logan said. "You aren't. Sebastian is a terrible person. That's what people like him do. Slowly take you away from your friends and family. Then his friends and family become yours. Your hobbies must be his hobbies. You go places with him or not at all. It's death by a thousand cuts. You don't see it coming."

Ava lifted her head. "Wow. That's exactly it. How do you know that's what he did?"

Logan shrugged and rose from the side of the mattress. "Let's just say my father was a piece of work. There's a reason my mom divorced him, other than the gambling." He snatched a pair of black sweats off the floor and pulled them on, neglecting to put on underwear first. "She was a shell of herself by the time she found the strength to tell him to leave. I don't know how, or what the last straw was, but she did it."

Ava sat up, giving him her attention. "How old were you?"

"Eight." He threw a long-sleeve shirt over his head and yanked it down. "I thought the divorce was my fault. Typical kid shit. When I was much older, my mom finally told me how he treated her, and in hindsight, his behaviour was easy to see. But what eight-year-old recognizes narcissistic behaviour? They just see their dad being mean, or their mom being sad, and don't understand why." He sat on the bedside and kissed her shoulder. "What happened with Sebastian is not your fault."

"I don't think I've ever heard Logan share so

much. Three-way sex must really soften you up, eh?" Roman teased.

"Shut up, Banks." Logan chucked a pillow at Roman's head, catching him full in the face.

Roman laughed and flipped him off.

Logan refocused on Ava. "The point is—I get it. It's hard to start over, and it's your choice, but we're here if you're ready."

She wrapped the sheets around her middle. "There really isn't anything tying me to Ottawa anymore. My apartment, sure, but that's easy to deal with. My family's in Toronto, so we already live in different cities."

"Are you considering it?" Roman asked, careful to keep the excitement out of his voice until she made a definitive decision.

"I…am considering it," she echoed back.

"Fuck yeah! That's my girl." Roman shot up and embraced her so quickly, they toppled onto the bed. He kissed her anywhere he could find. Her neck, her lips, her chest, her shoulders.

She broke out in a fit of giggles, pushing at him playfully. "Get off! You're too heavy."

He ignored her and pressed his body flush against hers, pinning her to the bed.

"You're squishing me!" she laughed.

The feel of her squirming under him was quickly getting him going again. He grew hard against her thigh, and his kisses became heated and needy.

"Roman," Ava warned between kisses.

"One more time, love. One more." He sucked at one of her breasts, swirling his tongue over her nipple.

Her breath caught in her throat, and she hummed against him.

"I'm going to make us supper," Logan called, already halfway across the room. "Tidy my bed when you're done." He shut the door behind him.

She caressed his beard and whispered, "You need to be gentle with me this time around."

"Anything for you, love," he promised, pushing inside her with a sigh.

She was tight and warm around him.

Like the promise of a future.

Like heaven.

Like home.

AVA

Never in her life had she had so much sex. Everything was sore. And by everything, she meant ev-er-y-thing. She would have to ban the guys from touching her for the next three days. Somehow, she didn't think that would go over well.

"What are we having?" she asked, inhaling the

scent of garlic and oregano in the air. "It smells amazing."

"Have a seat," Logan instructed. "And you'll see."

She sat next to Roman at the dining table and watched as Logan put together two meals and brought the plates to them.

"Chicken Florentine with sun-dried tomatoes and spinach. Nothing fancy. Just good comfort food."

"Nothing fancy? Is that a joke?" Her eyes bulged at the meal before her. The array of colours made her mouth water.

"Oh trust me, you haven't seen anything yet. The food he's made you so far pales compared to his true cooking ability." Roman praised his best friend, appearing like a proud papa bear.

"That's enough," Logan muttered, fixing his own plate and joining them.

"He doesn't take compliments very well, in case you haven't noticed. But he's always in the kitchen doing something new," he said with admiration.

"It's a good way to blow off steam. Gives me time to process the day," Logan added.

Ava took a bite and made a slightly sexual sound. Both men glanced at her, eyebrows raised.

"Sorry. It's that good."

Roman's laugh rumbled through the quiet house, and she saw a smile tug the corner of Logan's lips. One day, she'd get a big old grin out of him.

"Listen, Ava," Logan said, a hint of caution in his tone. "I need to tell you something."

Nothing good ever started with those six words. Alarm bells rang in her head. He better not be backing out of this relationship. Especially after their amazing, life-altering, three-way sex. No way in hell.

She put her fork and knife back on the table. "What is it?"

He cleared his throat. "I did something I shouldn't have. I need to be accountable, and I want you to know I'm sorry. I never thought we'd get together, and…" His gaze dropped to his lap.

What the hell did he do? "Okay, you're scaring me. You need to tell me what you did right now, so I don't start freaking out more than I already am."

Roman nodded at Logan, encouraging him to continue. Obviously, he was in the know when she was not. Why would he keep something from her?

"When you first arrived, I opened your phone, found Sebastian's voice message, and sent it to myself. I listened to some of it without your permission."

Her forehead wrinkled. "Some of it?"

"I couldn't get through the whole thing," he rushed out. "It made me so fucking angry."

"Oh." A million questions danced in her head. But only one mattered. "Why did you need to hear it?"

"I…needed to know what was so bad that you'd leave home and come here." He sighed. "Also, I'm an asshole and was bitter about you and Roman clicking so fast. I wanted to be on the inside, too."

Ava nodded, processing his words. He did this behind her back, yes, but they weren't together when he did. She pictured him sneaking off to listen to the message, alone in his room. All the things she wanted in a sexual partner. All the things she admitted after two years of being with someone. Was that how he knew exactly what to say to her to get her off? She couldn't believe that was the reason for their chemistry. The idea was too painful.

"Ava?" Logan asked, worry in his eyes.

"Exactly how much did you listen to?" She had to know. Everything he did with her was so perfectly depraved. If the reason was the voice message, and not just how he truly was with her, she couldn't handle that.

"I made it halfway through and stopped. I swear on my fucking life, Ava. I stopped."

Half. He listened to half of it. Not everything, but enough to know what to say and do. "So everything we did together…was it only because of the message?"

He rose from his chair and kneeled at her side, taking her hands in his. "No, sweetheart. I heard some things, sure. But that's not why we have what we have." He placed his hand on her heart, and she looked into his eyes. "If anything, it gave me the push to let myself be with you the way I wanted to. The way you needed me to."

A defining moment was taking place right in front of her. Logan was literally on his knees, apologizing to her. Something she never thought she'd witness him do. His voice was sincere, and she didn't doubt his honesty.

So what was she to do? Get upset about something she couldn't change? Or accept that he'd made a mistake and owned it?

Already, she realized it had to be the three of them to work. Roman was her rock, her sweet man. And Logan was her protector, her dominator. Both were necessary in this relationship, and she didn't want one slip to impede that.

"I forgive you," she said, taking Logan's face in her hand. "Thank you for telling me. But please, don't go behind my back like that again. I can't handle any more trust issues, okay?"

Logan closed his eyes and leaned into her touch. "I promise, Ava. Never again." He turned his face and kissed her palm. "Never."

"I know." She was thankful for his candor. That he didn't hide it from her any longer or use it against her. They were learning as they went, and that was okay. "Now, go sit down so we can eat this mouthwatering food you made."

"So I was thinking," she said around bites of chicken. "I'll need to break my lease. I've lived there so long, I don't remember what my contract says, so it might be awhile before I can get out of it. At the same time, I should be trying to find a place to rent in Little Greenfield. Do you guys know anyone with a space?"

Logan shook his head. "Nonsense."

"You're living with us," Roman stated, as if it was the most obvious thing in the world.

"I can't live with you. We barely—"

"Know each other," the two guys said at the same time.

"So you've said, Ava. More than a few times." Logan grabbed the wine bottle, uncorked it, and poured them each a glass.

"My parents got married after four weeks. Did I ever tell you that?" Roman mused.

Ava tilted her head. "Four weeks? That's not far off how long I've known you both."

"Exactly."

She took another bite, careful not to derail their conversation with any obvious noises of pleasure because of how ridiculously tasty it was. Probably the best chicken she'd ever had. Who would've thought Logan was such a master in the kitchen? She knew he was good, but not this good. Having someone cook for her was comforting.

"And if this all blows up in our faces?" she asked.

"It won't," they both said, again in unison. Like their brains were connected by an invisible wire.

"How are you both so confident? Logan, you didn't even like me until like…four days ago."

"Not true. I liked you the second I saw you. But I couldn't let myself admit it." He took a swig of wine.

"Listen, Ava." Roman set down his silverware and gave her his full attention. "Logan and I have discussed it. We'll add another room to the back house. Then you can have your own space."

Her hand flew to her chest. "You'd do that for me?"

Roman nodded. "You know what I'm going to say, don't you?"

Grateful tears filled her eyes. "Anything for me?"

He gave her hand a squeeze. "Anything for you."

She rolled the idea around in her mind, letting it percolate. Moving to Little Greenfield. Living with Roman and Logan. Permanently. The idea definitely terrified and thrilled her at the same time. Here were two good men—dreamy men—who accepted her for who she was. They wanted to live with her, be with her, share her in every way.

It was so different to how she lived her life until that point. But a change would be good. New boyfriends—plural. New town, new house, new…job?

No way she would let Roman and Logan foot the bill for everything. She needed to contribute just as much as they did. "What am I going to do for work?"

Roman's face lit up. "Well, we have an idea, don't we, Logey? Didn't I say this would work out?"

Logan pointed his fork at him. "Not that I had any doubts to begin with."

She glanced between them. "What are you two talking about?"

"Well"—a shit-eating grin spread across Roman's face—"Logan handles construction. He built the bed and breakfast, with a little help from me. I already own and run the pub, which I'll be taking a step back from, so I know the administrative side of a business. We need someone who knows how to market a bed and breakfast. Create advertisements, run campaigns, bring in customers. You've already started helping us with that, but does it sound like something you'd be interested in long-term?"

Ava beamed. Her chest felt lighter than it had in days. "I could do that. I could definitely do that. There's one problem, though."

Roman's eyes narrowed. "What is it? I know it's a start-up, but we will make enough to pay us all eventually, and until then, we can—"

"Not that, silly." Ava giggled. "How can I market a bed and breakfast with no name?"

He rolled his eyes and shook his head. "You scared me for a second. I've suggested plenty of names. It's this one"—he pointed a finger in Logan's direction—"who won't agree on any of them."

"Can I hear some?"

"No way," Logan said. "They're way too terrible to be uttered aloud in this house again. Don't embarrass yourself." He gave Roman a pointed stare.

Now she had to know. "They can't be that bad."

"They are. Not a word, Banks."

"We'll think of something, love. Don't you worry."

Worry was the furthest thing from her mind. She could have a life here. A real, enjoyable, love-filled life in Little Greenfield. The town was so much smaller than the big city she was used to, but that wasn't a bad thing.

Adorable shops lined Main Street. A fishing competition brought in tourists. She'd have to figure out new events for other times in the year to bring more people here. The locals would appreciate more business on the regular, no doubt. There was good food, good drinks—that gin could bring in a crowd all on its own—and good people. Marketing would be a cinch.

The B&B was gorgeous. Rustic and cozy, and she would make sure it had the best amenities a guest could hope for. Not only would guests love it here, but she would too. She already did. This felt like home. It had from the first day she set foot inside, but she hadn't realized it then.

A newfound energy coursed through her veins. Brainstorming a winter event to draw people to town, and starting an advertising campaign would be her top priorities.

"Can we make a plan tonight? Of what we need to do in order to get to opening day?" She leaned forward eagerly, hoping they'd agree to get going as soon as possible.

Roman nodded. "That's a great idea. We can see what we have left to do and nail down a marketing strategy for our grand opening in January. What do you say, Logan?"

"I had a different idea for how I'd spend the night." Logan laced his fingers through hers. The heat in his eyes sent a clear message.

"Down, boy. I am way too spent to have any kind of *different idea* happen to me."

"Fine," Logan huffed, removing his hand from hers. "We'll spend the night planning for the business. But my idea was going to be way more fun."

Ava gathered the dishes and clicked her tongue at him on the way to the sink. "Maybe we can try your idea next week."

"Next week?" Logan slumped in his seat.

She burst out laughing. Roman's throaty chuckle joined hers.

"Okay, not next week, but give me a few days. You both ruined me today, and I need to recuperate." She fixed him with a sharp stare.

Logan threw up his hands in defeat. "I relent."

"Besides, I'm sexy when I talk business. Just you wait and see," she teased, winking at him from the kitchen.

Chapter Twenty

AVA

"Here's how it'll go," Ava said from the armchair in the corner of the living room, a pad of paper and pen in hand. "Each time we determine a specific point for the B&B's marketing strategy, I'll take off an item of clothing. Once there's nothing left, we can call it a night."

"And by *call it a night*, you mean..." Logan prompted, shamelessly grabbing his dick.

Ava rolled her eyes but couldn't keep the smile off her face. "I mean go to sleep. Oh, and no touching. Only looking."

"You can't just get naked and expect us not to—"

Roman smacked Logan in the chest. "That sounds more than fair. I'm down for a strip tease with a side of work."

Still, Logan seemed surly at the prospect of no sex.

She fixed him with her stare. "Tits and work, or no tits and work?"

He crossed his arms. "Fine. Tits and work. Like there's another answer."

Ava grinned and uncapped her pen. "Perfect. Let's start with an easy one. The B&B needs a name."

Logan sighed heavily. "That is *not* an easy one. Roman won't consider anything that isn't pun-based."

"It's not that I won't consider it. You haven't suggested anything to compete with my ideas, Logey," he teased.

"Can I finally hear these names?"

"No—"

"Yes! I have so many." Roman cut Logan off in a rush to answer her. "The Best Bread and Breakfast, Muffin But Beds, The Great Eggscape, Toast of the Town Inn, The Flapjack Nap Shack. I can keep going, if you want."

Logan grimaced. "Oh my God, Banks. That's more than enough."

She chuckled. "Those are amazing, Roman. Do they speak to our target demographic?"

"People? Yeah, I think most people like puns, save for Grumpy Pants over here." He shoved his best friend on the shoulder.

Logan's gaze flicked upward as he shook his head.

"We'll be lucky to get Ava's shirt off at the rate we're going."

"What distinct group of people? Who do we specifically want to target as our main audience for the B&B?"

The two glanced at each other, and Logan answered, "I don't think we considered that. We just thought anyone who wants to stay would be welcome to stay."

"The business needs a niche," she explained. "We'll do better if we know who we're trying to appeal to. Are we looking to serve an older or younger clientele? Do we want families staying here or couples? Is this a place for relaxation or adventure? Not only should the name of the B&B speak to that, but it will help guide my marketing strategy."

Roman's shoulders slumped. "I guess a pun-based name isn't the best option."

She hated seeing him look defeated. "Not necessarily. A pun that speaks to our target audience could work, but we need to nail that down."

He nodded. "Okay. Let's answer those questions."

Logan folded his arms across his chest. "And you need to take a piece of clothing off for each answer, or I'm going to lose my mind."

She tried her best not to appear too smug. "Deal. Are we looking to serve a fifty plus age range, new adults, or more in the thirty to forty demographic?"

"Thirty to forty," Logan and Roman answered at the same time.

Ava grabbed the hem of the shirt she'd thrown on before supper that evening. Dragging it upwards as slowly as possible, arching her back, she revealed her emerald lace bra.

Roman hummed his approval, sweeping his gaze over her torso.

Logan clenched his fists. "Fuck, Ava. You're doing this to me on purpose, aren't you?"

She smirked at him. "I can neither confirm nor deny that."

"Next question," Roman urged.

"Will our B&B serve families or couples?"

"Easy. Couples. Shorts off, sweetheart," Logan ordered.

"Hold on," Roman put his hand out. "Why not families?"

Logan scoffed. "I can think of a handful of reasons. First, I don't want a bunch of rugrats getting their shit everywhere. Second, crying babies waking other patrons in the middle of the night? No, thank you. Last, I imagine some families might have an issue staying with polyamorous owners."

Roman's mouth dropped open. "That's a lot of reasons off the top of your head."

He shrugged. "I've thought about it before. Kids just aren't my thing."

She nodded. "Honestly, I'm with Logan. And I

think this place would make a charming couples retreat. Are you okay with that, Roman?"

"I could go either way. Couples it is."

"Strip," Logan commanded.

She stood, slipping her thumbs inside the waistband of her sleep shorts, and dragged them down an inch at a time.

Roman gave a loud wolf whistle, so she threw the shorts to him.

Catching them in the air, he brought them to his face and inhaled. "I fucking love the smell of you."

She twirled on the spot, showing off her matching emerald lace g-string.

"You little tease," Logan growled.

She sat with her legs spread open. "Relaxation or adventure?" Sure, her pussy wasn't ready for another round with Roman and Logan yet, but that didn't mean she couldn't make them squirm.

"I've thought about this," Roman said. "There's not a lot of high-stakes adventuring around Little Greenfield, but there are plenty of cozy feel-good opportunities. We could even put a hot tub on the deck."

"Agreed. Take out your tits, sweetheart."

She clicked her tongue. "Do you actually agree, or do you just want my bra off?"

"Both. Take it off. Now." The intensity in Logan's eyes told her he wasn't messing around.

Reaching behind her, she unclasped her bra, and

let it drop onto her lap.

Logan sat forward and bit his fist.

"You're magnificent, love," Roman said, palming the bulge in his pants. "I need to see your pussy again. Ask us one more question."

She should've put socks on. Or a cardigan. Or any other item so she would've been able to play with them longer. But this was her last piece of clothing, and she wanted to make it count.

"What sets this B&B apart from others? Why should guests stay here, and not anywhere else?"

"It's local," Roman stated, staring at her tits.

"Why does that matter?" she challenged.

"We know the area. We know the people who live here. We built the place with our own two hands. Any money made here will be invested back into the community. We're not a soulless chain hotel with a faceless CEO. We *are* Little Greenfield."

She couldn't keep the pride off of her face. "I love that, Roman. Local founders with local knowledge." She scribbled his words down in her notepad, then focused on Logan. "Anything to add?"

"We'll be a boutique experience. Intimate feel. Cozy aesthetic. Personalized service. Curated getaway packages."

"Yes to all of that. What kind of getaway packages were you thinking of?"

"No more questions, sweetheart. Underwear off."

She batted her eyelashes. "Don't I get a *please*?"

"Please, love. I'm dying over here." Roman's pleading gaze met her own. The desperation in his eyes was a boost to her ego. She made him look that hungry, no touching necessary.

She sauntered to the staircase, aware that their eyes followed with each step. "Goodnight, boys," she called, ascending the first three steps. "See you in the morning."

"Don't you fucking dare." Logan's voice was low and dangerous. She didn't need to see his face to know he was serious.

Ava turned around to face them, skimming her palms over her breasts. "Are you going to beg?"

Roman shot off the couch and landed at her feet on the staircase. "Please take it off, love. Please let us see." He reached out to grasp her leg.

She pulled away. "Tsk, tsk. No touching, Roman. Remember?"

He tucked his hands dutifully behind his back. "Just one peek. Let me go to bed with the picture of your perfect pussy in my mind."

She locked eyes with Logan. "Are you going to beg, too?"

"I don't beg."

Pursing her lips in a mock-pout, she said, "I guess I'll have to go to bed. Or maybe I'll take Roman with me, since he's being such a good boy, begging on his knees."

Logan stood. The muscles in his jaw twitched. "I

don't beg."

"Too bad." She turned her attention to Roman and ran her fingers through his brunette locks. "Sounds like you get a private show," she said with a wink.

"Not a fucking chance." He joined them on the steps. Glaring at Ava, he repeated, "I don't beg."

"You do tonight." She placed her hand on his shoulder and slowly pushed him down. He didn't fight her, and sank to his knees beside Roman.

"Take them off. We need to see that pretty cunt before we're done here."

"That sounded like a demand. Want to try again?" She was enjoying this far too much. She wasn't the dominating type, but there was something about seeing Logan and Roman on their knees, staring up at her, aching for her pussy, that drove her wild.

Logan looked down and exhaled before meeting her gaze and saying, "Please take that goddamn fucking g-string off."

"Why should I?" She was being a brat, but the opportunity to toy with Logan was too appealing to pass up.

"Because you fucking promised us we could see your greedy cunt. If you don't deliver, I'm going to rip that g-string off you myself and—"

She cleared her throat. "That doesn't sound like begging." Grabbing Roman's head, she shoved it against her pussy, and he let out a groan. "Beg me, Logan, or I'm taking Roman to my room."

"Fuck!" he yelled, bowing his head. "Please take off your g-string, Ava. Shove it in my mouth. Wrap it around my throat. Do what you want with me. Just please let me see your pussy before I go fucking feral."

"Look at me, Logan," she commanded, releasing Roman from his place against her.

Logan's gaze met hers, and she slid the emerald fabric down her legs, nudging it to him with her foot. He grabbed the underwear and shoved it into his back pocket.

"Sit down, love. Spread your legs. We want to see every inch of you," Roman crooned from his place at her feet.

She obeyed, knowing putting herself on display would test their restraint.

Her fingers drifted to her clit in full view of her two men, and she allowed her head to relax. She sensed their stares, and could hear them panting as they watched. She had to give them something. "I said you couldn't touch me. I never said you couldn't touch yourselves."

A rustle of clothing. Their hands pumping on their cocks joined her own slick sounds of self-pleasure. Lifting her head, she witnessed Roman and Logan fucking their hands to the sight of her. She watched them watch her, and a fresh wave of arousal coated her fingertips.

Fuck not letting them touch her. She'd denied them enough.

"Lick my cunt," she ordered. "Both of you. Together. Right now."

They crawled to her and spread her legs as wide as they could go. Dipping down together, they ran their tongues over her pussy, lapping at her, while stroking themselves with their free hands. Her cunt rippled at the sight of their tongues touching, eating her together, tasting each other while tasting her.

"Yes, yes, fuck yes," she cried, raking her hands into their hair, bucking into their faces. Their tongues dancing together against her pussy was the hottest thing she'd ever seen. She jerked against them, her orgasm crashing through her in a sharp wave, arousal spilling into their mouths and down her thighs.

"That's our filthy fucking slut," Logan groaned against her, sliding his tongue to her ass, and licking her there.

"She's a needy thing. One mouth isn't good enough for her," Roman moaned into her cunt, pressing his tongue inside her pussy.

"Come on me," she managed to say. One last command for her two men.

They straightened, working their cocks for her. Both of their faces glistened with her wetness.

"I'm gonna coat your tight little asshole with my cum, sweetheart," Logan growled.

"And I'm gonna claim your pussy hole, love."

Roman's gravelly voice traveled down her spine.

Their bodies shuddered together, like they were of one mind, and hot cum erupted onto her. Seeing Roman and Logan orgasm together left her reeling. Especially after their tongues had licked into each other's mouths while on her pussy.

Reaching down, she ran her fingers down her clit and through their cum, mixing it together. "So good," she sobbed. "So fucking good."

"You're going to wear us to bed, and nothing else," Logan growled. "Understand, sweetheart?"

She nodded, lost in the euphoria of their releases and the sight of them standing over her, cocks spent and chests heaving.

No doubt about it, this was what she wanted.

Roman and Logan. They were hers. They were home.

Alone in her guest room with Roman and Logan's cum dripping down her thighs, Ava stretched out underneath the heavy quilt on her bed. Though it wouldn't be her bed for much longer. After promising more three-way sex as soon as possible, Roman and Logan allowed her to go to bed alone for the night.

She had so much to process. The last ten days had been life-changing. Better than she ever could've dreamed. But life wasn't a dream, and she had to be practical and figure out the little details, not just moon over the two ridiculously good-looking men currently sleeping downstairs.

Details like where was she going to sleep once they opened? Adding a room onto the back house seemed like a huge disruption to their timeline. But she did want her own space. Staying in one of the guest suites permanently was not an option.

But starting construction on a fresh addition would set them back, and they wouldn't open in three months like planned. She needed to figure out an alternative that worked for everybody. Somewhere she could have her own space, but not cause a great deal of construction or renovation. Though she knew they'd tell her they wouldn't mind. Anything for her.

She rolled over to stare out the glass balcony doors. The stars were in rare form tonight. Shining so bright, she could see them from her bed. This was a sight she'd never tire of. The sky didn't sparkle like this in the city. Too much light pollution blocked out the night sky entirely.

Every moment she spent with her two men, her feelings grew deeper. Moving in with them was the right choice. For them to be together. She was eager to get started on this new life, but she needed to end the lease on her apartment. And get her car. Then change all her personal information to a new address. Break the news to her parents that she was dating, and moving in with, two men. How they'd take that was anyone's guess. The to-do list was daunting, but exhilarating.

She stared at her notebook on the bedside table. She came to Little Greenfield to figure out what she wanted in a partner. What positives did she hope for? What negatives needed avoiding? But Roman and Logan had shown her in real time what two devoted, caring, healthy partners looked like. She didn't need her pros and cons list anymore.

A new life. A fresh start. A chance to do it right this time. Focus on her and the people she loved. Take pride in being in a healthy relationship. Fuck like animals and explore every one of her desires. Demand what she was worth and give all of herself to the ones who made her their universe.

Now was the time to contact her friends. Would they still consider her a friend? Putting it off any longer wasn't an option.

She missed Layla and Brittany terribly. They were the ones who held on the longest. Tried and tried again to get through to her. But she never listened.

Sebastian had eroded her self-worth, isolated her, and made her dependent on him for any kind of validation. She'd lost everyone close to her because of his actions and her inaction. Taking responsibility was a crucial first step in mending her friendships. Time to stop being idle and take control. Tomorrow, she'd reach out. She'd apologize. She'd make amends.

Tomorrow, her life started again.

Chapter Twenty-One

AVA

"Why did Roman want to meet us here?" she asked Logan, who was sitting across from her at a window table in Wakin' & Bacon, tapping his foot and glancing at his watch every few seconds.

"He didn't say."

Maria came over with their to-go order: three coffees, two Roman Specials, and a Montreal smoked meat breakfast bagel. The heavenly mix of sweet and salty aromas wafted around Ava. She'd been in Little Greenfield for five weeks now, and Maria made her sickly sweet coffee as soon as she set foot in the door. One of the many things she appreciated about Little Greenfield was how friendly the residents were. They took care of their own and the people who visited.

"He better hurry," Logan grumbled, sipping his

black coffee. "If I don't leave soon, I'll be late getting to Elora. It's a four-hour drive."

"And you'll be gone for a week?" Her heart hurt to think of Logan leaving.

He softened his tone. "If everything goes to plan, only five days."

Logan was going to work for a couple who'd recently retired and wanted a one-room cabin on their property. They hoped to earn an income from tourists who normally visited for day trips. He'd told her that when he was on a build, he could be gone for weeks at a time. Maybe she'd be able to go with him on longer projects. Help with the finishings and design.

Concern marred his brow. "Why the frown, sweetheart?"

"Just thinking about you leaving. I don't want to be without you."

"I'm a text away. Or a phone call. Or a…video chat." He smirked at her with a not-so-subtle suggestion gleaming in his eye.

She traced a finger over the back of his hand. "Oh, there will be plenty of *video chats*, I promise."

"Yeah?" He leaned forward, and his voice lowered so only she could hear him. "And what will you do for me in these videos, Ava?"

"Anything you want."

"Touch yourself?"

"Yes."

"Play with your toys while I stroke myself?"

"Yes." Her pulse quickened.

"Ride Roman's cock for me?"

She licked her lips at the idea. "You want to watch that?"

"You know I like to watch, sweetheart."

"I like when you watch me."

He winked. "I know."

She sighed. "I'm going to miss you."

He reclined in his chair. "I'll miss you too. But this will be a good trial run. Once I'm away on longer jobs, it'll just be you and Roman in the house. Then what are you going to do without my good-nature and extreme positivity?"

His sarcasm made her snort. "I think I'll miss your cooking more than your upbeat attitude," she teased.

Logan's eyes brightened at her praise. "I know I'm fantastic, but Roman's not a terrible cook."

"Maybe I could help with bigger projects?" she ventured. "Accompany you on your travels? You know I have the skills."

"We can definitely work something out. I'd love that, sweetheart."

"In the meantime, I'll make do with Roman's cooking. Or my own." She grimaced.

"You can always go to the pub and have Megan whip something up for you," Logan offered.

"We chatted for a bit when I was there the other day. I'd like to get to know her more."

"And she'd be lucky to get to know you." He graced her with a genuine smile, which was a rare sight. A cocky smile? Sure. A smug smirk? Always. But an authentic smile from him made her heart quiver.

She was determined to make friends here. It'd been a while, and she felt awkward and out of practice, but dammit, she was motivated.

Last week, Brittany had thanked her for calling, but said—in the nicest possible way—that she wasn't interested in re-kindling their friendship. Her rejection had hurt but been understandable.

Layla, on the other hand, was thrilled to hear from her. Contacting her after calling Brittany, and essentially being dumped, was nerve-wracking. But they proceeded to talk for two hours—updating each other on life, love, and everything in between.

Layla wanted to be their first guest at the B&B. She'd booked in for opening weekend while they were on the phone, stating she'd be there with bells on, her new boyfriend in tow. Layla hadn't lost faith in her, and it filled her with joy. She even wanted to support Ava's new life in Little Greenfield. It was a good start.

No, a great start.

"He's here." Logan motioned out the window to where Roman's truck pulled up to the curb.

She grabbed Roman's flat white—slightly better than Logan's black coffee, but not sweet enough in her opinion—and followed Logan outside.

"What's all the secrecy about? Why did we

need to meet you here and not at home?" Logan asked as he opened the front door for Ava, then climbed in the backseat. "Are you finally giving Ava the bill for her initial eight days at the B&B?"

She snorted. "I think I paid for that in other ways, thank you very much."

"You mean the sex?" he snickered.

Stretching her arm into the back, she slapped his leg. "I mean the work I've put in getting the bed and breakfast ready to open."

Logan chuckled and slid his legs out of her reach. "So what is it, Banks?"

"It's a surprise." Roman's smile was the biggest she'd ever seen.

"I think we guessed as much," Ava said, leaning in to kiss him.

Throwing the truck in gear, he headed straight for the B&B. Calling it *the B&B* was getting old, and the marketing materials she was putting together were useless without a name.

"When Logan gets back, can we sit down and name this place? It can't be the B&B forever."

"Agreed," Logan said from the backseat. "Or Ava and I could name it right now. Banks is the one that keeps impeding our progress with his pun-derful name ideas."

Ava mock-gasped at him. "You did not just make a pun about puns."

He put his palm on his heart. "I apologize. It'll never happen again."

Roman shifted in his seat, glancing at her, then Logan, then back at the road. The grin on his face was too large. Too wide. She swore he was about to burst.

She squinted her eyes at him. "Roman…what did you do?"

"I may have, uh, named the bed and breakfast," he said quietly.

"What?" Logan yelled, lurching forward and poking his face between the front seats. "You did what, you big oaf?"

"I named it."

Logan cursed. "Named it as in you filled out some official paperwork or wrote it on a sticky note and stuck it on the fridge?"

"Named it as in I commissioned two laser-cut steel signs the day after Ava said she'd stay. That's when I thought of it. I may have filled out a few official documents, too." His sheepish tone didn't minimize the excitement in his eyes.

"And you had us meet you at the coffee shop because…" Logan probed.

"Because I installed the signs at both ends of our driveway while you were out, and I wanted it to be a surprise. Like I said."

"Shit," Logan said, resting his face in his hand.

"It's going to be named something like The Egg-cellent B&B or Here Today, Scone Tomorrow."

She tried to contain the amusement bubbling in her chest, but couldn't manage it any longer. Her laughter filled the cab, along with a few snorts.

"Hey—you have to live and work there too, sweetheart. You really want to spend your days marketing a place named No Place Butter than Here?"

"Oh my gosh. Roman, please tell me that's it." She wiped away a tear. "Everyone loves a good butter pun."

Logan slumped back in his seat, letting his head thump against the rear window. "We're screwed."

"Make all the jokes you want, but the name is perfect. I promise you." His tone was pure confidence. He didn't appear to be rattled by their joking.

Ava patted Roman's forearm. "I believe you."

His eyes brightened. "You do?"

She nodded. "If you were confident enough to get signs made and file with the registry, then yes, I believe you."

"Am I the one rational person in this truck?" Logan piped in. "His track record is terrible."

"Well, you're about to find out if I struck out again or if I hit gold. Close your eyes."

"I am not closing my—"

"Do it, Logan."

With a reluctant sigh, Logan closed his eyes, and Ava joined him. She felt the truck turn onto the dirt road driveway that led to the bed and breakfast. The truck slowed to a stop.

"Okay. I need you to both keep your eyes closed as you get out. Ava, I'll help you."

Roman's door squeaked open, then slammed shut. A few moments later, her door opened, and Roman's familiar gentle but firm hands led her onto the ground safely.

"I'll make my own way," Logan grumbled behind them. "Don't worry about me."

"Here, take Ava's hand." Roman put one of her hands in Logan's, but kept hold of the other. "Now, walk this way. A few more steps. Open your eyes."

It took a second to focus properly, then she saw the beautiful sign a few feet in front of her. A metal stand was anchored in the ground, with a large sign hanging off a crossbar, swaying ever-so-slightly in the breeze. Three pine trees were cut into the black steel —one for each of them.

Her breath caught in her throat, and tears burned her eyes as she read the sign.

Three Hearts Hideaway.

"What do you think?" Roman asked. He'd been quiet, letting them take it in and digest.

"It's absolutely perfect." She let go of Logan's hand and threw her arms around Roman's neck, kissing the delicate flowers etched there. "I love it. But are you sure? What if we don't work out? What if the three of us being together is too hard? What if—?"

"Ava," he said, voice smooth and soothing in her ear. "No what-ifs. I knew the moment I saw you that you were mine. I have no doubts. It's time to stop worrying and embrace what we are." He leaned down and kissed her. A slow, sensual kiss that invaded her senses and left her breathless. Drawing back, he said, "Can you do that for me, love?"

His tawny eyes filled with something she was a little too scared to name. It was too early. But the look warmed her to the core. "I can do that, Roman."

She shifted in his arms. Logan stared at the sign, arms crossed, with a wrinkle in his brow. His default expression. Grumpy, pissed-off, angry-looking Logan was really just normal Logan. She smiled at the progress she'd made getting through his very high walls.

"Logan?" She took a step toward him. "Do you like it?"

He pivoted abruptly and pointed his finger in Roman's face. "You did a good fucking job, Banks."

Roman exhaled and his booming laugh followed, rumbling through the trees. "Thanks, Logey. You scared me for a second there."

"You deserved it." He smirked, satisfied with himself.

"I won't deny that."

She wrapped one arm around Roman, the other around Logan. "I'm so glad you like it, too."

This felt right. Here. Between her two men. She

breathed in the crisp forest air. A brisk autumn breeze blew through the trees.

The warmth of summer was always welcome, and always gone too soon. But the leaves were changing from green to the glorious golds and crimsons of fall. This year, she wouldn't miss the warmth.

Change was good.

Change was necessary.

Change was inevitable.

Even though it was a bigger risk than any she'd ever taken, this change was meant to be. How did she get so lucky? To have a tattooed teddy bear who'd give her the world on a silver platter, and a fierce protector who allowed her to relish in the darker sides of herself?

Fully accepting herself as she was would be a long road. Deprogramming her negative thoughts would take time. Maybe she'd seek a therapist.

But for now—for right now—everything she needed to start healing, moving on, and accepting herself was right here with Roman and Logan and their bed and breakfast. They were who she wanted, and she was confident in that.

Logan took her hand and tugged her down the driveway to the cabin. His eyes were hungry, and she didn't need to be a psychic to know what was going on in his head. "This calls for a celebration."

"What were you thinking?" she asked, knowing full well what was on his mind.

"I'm sure you can figure that out on your own," Roman whispered in her ear, trailing so closely behind her that she felt the heat radiating off of him.

"Logan, aren't you going to be late getting to Elora?" she teased.

"I can spare thirty or forty minutes." The hum in his voice was dangerous.

The three of them hurried up the steps and to the front door. Logan's hands groped her hips. Roman's mouth was on her neck. She breathed them in, relaxing into their touch, reaching for more. Lips on her lips. Skin on her skin. Hands tugged at her clothes. Her fingers tangled in Roman's hair and wrapped around Logan's thick forearm.

As her two men ushered her inside, she turned, wanting one more glimpse of the sign naming the property.

Three Hearts Hideaway.

Her chest ached with an overwhelming feeling of comfort. She needed Roman and Logan, but they needed her, too. Wanted her. She was a part of them, and they were a part of her. Three hearts joined together.

Yes.

It truly was the perfect name.

Epilogue

Six Months Later

AVA

Winter was almost at an end. The bite in the air had lessened, the sun on her cheeks felt warm, and puddles had replaced the piles of snow. Each year, the Canadian winter reminded her how much she enjoyed the Canadian summer.

Not that she minded winter in Little Greenfield. Even when the weather was cold, the town's atmosphere was cozy, warm. Over the Christmas season, twinkling white lights had hung outside the shops, and cute banners with winter adornments had decorated the light posts. She had especially enjoyed the one with the snowman couple holding hands.

Walking down Main Street toward The White Pine Pub, she missed the decorations. Hopefully, they'd display new ones now that the season was changing.

Roman and Logan had kept insisting on giving her a personal space, but she didn't want them bogged down with the extra construction of adding a room to the owner's suites. They'd settled on adding her own private and separate tiny house behind Three Hearts Hideaway.

It functioned as her bedroom and office with a small bathroom and kitchenette, though she hardly ever used the latter. She'd grown addicted to Logan's drool-worthy cooking.

She passed by Wakin' & Bacon and plastered her face to the glass window, peering inside. She locked eyes with Maria and gave a quick wave, happy to see her face, and continued on toward the pub.

With the help of her favourite residents, she'd organized Frost Fest, a two-week winter festival in January. Her personal goal was to pack the B&B with guests. Her goal for the town was to help the local businesses make extra income.

Layla helped her flesh out the Frost Fest idea. They had a weekly phone date where they'd discussed ways to bring more people to the area.

They also talked about more delectable topics… like the men in their lives. Hearing all of Layla's stories about exploring her exhibitionist kink with her boyfriend, James, was freeing. She loved being able to share about Roman and Logan without judgement. But mostly they brainstormed ideas for the winter festival.

Well, maybe not mostly.

Fifty-fifty.

A frozen-over Kawawaymog Lake was perfect for figure skating and hockey games. As part of the festival, they'd organized an ice-fishing competition. And Main Street was closed to traffic each evening and filled with outdoor seating, fire pits, and food stations. Maria had a stand with her famous Wakin' & Bacon alfajores. Dean sold authentic Canadian maple syrup taffy, poured right on a fresh bed of snow in front of his Drug Mart. Jack had a booth with samples of his gin. Roman offered a discount at his pub for anyone who stayed at Three Hearts Hideaway or The Quiet Shore Hotel. Logan created a snowshoe path from the town to their property and Ava added it to an activity pamphlet she made for visitors.

She'd heavily marketed and advertised the festival, and it paid off. They were booked solid for those two weeks and had to turn guests away. Gertie had the same problem, and what a good problem it was. Guests continued to arrive during the next few months, having heard the positive word from their friends and family.

Next week would be six months since she arrived in Little Greenfield on a whim. A rash decision that turned into the best of her life. She shook her head as she walked through the doors to Roman's pub.

"Over here, darling!" Gertie called, waving a soft and wrinkled hand her way. She was sporting bright opal teardrop earrings with a matching bracelet today. "I already ordered us drinks."

Ava pretended to be affronted, placing a palm on her chest. "Gertie, it's three in the afternoon."

She playfully waved her off. "Oh, it's five o'clock somewhere."

"Can't argue with that. What are we having?"

"Spiced hot rum toddies. Few days left to enjoy a warm drink like this. Spring is on the way, dear." She slid the glass to the other side of the booth as Ava took her seat and removed her toque.

"Speaking of spring…" she hinted, unable to keep the excitement from her face.

"Please tell me you're thinking of organizing some sort of spring fling for the town?" The eagerness in Gertie's eyes was contagious.

"I was playing around with the idea. You think the others would go along with it again?"

"Go along with it? Ava! You know how much they appreciated Frost Fest. You and your two fellas are breathing a new life into this town. Maria and Dean are hankering for the next thing. So am I. If only Harold were around to see it."

Joy radiated through her chest at Gertie's kind words. "Well, I think he would love what I'm planning for Spring Swing even more than Frost Fest." She winked and offered a supportive smile to the first friend she'd made in this small town.

"Spring Swing. I love it already." Gertie raised her cocktail for a quick cheer, and they clinked glasses.

"Hey, love," Roman said, leaving his place behind the bar and placing a kiss on her head. "Can I get you something to eat? And you Gertie?"

"I'm good with my hot toddy, hun. Thank you, though."

"I'd love a turkey club, if you can. With fries. And extra gravy."

Roman playfully rolled his eyes. "I should've known."

Ava grinned. "Anything for me, though, right?"

"Anything for you." With another quick kiss, he disappeared into the back room to relay her order to Megan in the kitchen.

Megan made the best turkey club with an added slice of avocado and a thin spread of pesto, just for her. After all, they'd become quite close-knit in the time she'd been there. Megan was now her closest friend, apart from Gertie, of course, who was currently beaming at her from across the booth.

Her cheeks flushed. "What?"

"Oh, nothing, darling. It's just so lovely seeing you both so happy. When you arrived in my hotel months ago, I never thought you'd end up living here. Let alone with a boyfriend! Well, two boyfriends." She chuckled.

"I'm still shocked you don't think it's strange."

Gertie shrugged her shoulders. "Who am I to judge? Love is love is love. When we find even a sliver of joy in this world, we need to hold it close to our hearts and let it bloom. We need to feed it and let it flourish. How that looks is different for everyone. You and your men are no different."

Ava blinked away the tears threatening to spill onto her cheeks. "You're a beautiful person, you know that, Gertie?"

She waved her away. "You flatter an old woman."

"Truly, you are. Thank you for your kind words and your friendship. That you, and so many others here, accept us and our relationship fills my soul in a way you can't imagine."

Gertie patted her hand. "I'm glad you're happy here in our little slice of life."

"I am, Gertie. I really am."

"Well, I best be returning to the hotel." She downed the rest of her drink. "It's almost time for late check-out."

"It was lovely to see you. Want to meet earlier next week so we have more time to chat?"

"Sounds good, dear. Here comes your other man," Gertie said, pointing to the front of the pub as she left.

Logan swaggered through the door, eyes locked on

her. No matter where she was, he always zeroed in on her in an instant. To a stranger, it would be unnerving. But to her? It sent her heart fluttering a mile-a-minute.

Every. Single. Time.

"Let's go, sweetheart." Logan held out his hand, waiting for hers.

"Go where? I haven't eaten yet."

Roman appeared from the back room, fidgeting with her takeout container. "Everything's packed up, including your extra gravy. Plus an extra, extra gravy."

Roman seemed like he was about to spill a giant secret, and Logan kept glaring at him. So typical of her men.

She playfully pointed a finger from one to the other. "What's going on, you two?"

"No more questions," Logan said, a bit too quickly. "Let's get in the truck and go."

Obviously, they'd planned something. Whatever it was, she didn't want to ruin it by prying too hard. She'd humour them.

"Take me away, boys."

The water of Kawawaymog Lake was smooth like a perfect pane of glass. Not a ripple in sight. Of course, they'd been to the lake numerous times, but this spot was different. Secluded and private. Almost like a secret retreat made just for them.

"This is breathtaking. Why haven't we come here before today?" Ava asked, taking a gulp from the thermos of homemade hot chocolate Logan had brought.

She snuggled between them, wrapped in a wool blanket, in the bed of Roman's pickup. Lined with blankets and pillows, the truck bed was surprisingly comfortable.

"Big Softy wanted to save it for a special occasion," Logan said, pulling her closer to his side.

"This is a special occasion?" She searched Roman's face for any hint of what was going on. Then she wracked her brain, trying to think if she'd missed something.

It wasn't her birthday. It wasn't either of their birthdays. Nothing stood out.

Roman exhaled slowly before saying, "We've been waiting a while to tell you this—"

"Only because Roman insisted we do it at the same time."

"Only because *Logan* needed a few more months than I did."

"Aw, don't say it like that. You're making me sound like a dick."

"Well…"

"Banks. Not the time."

Roman lifted his hands in surrender. "You're right, Logey. Not the time."

Ava waved the thermos in front of their faces. "I'm still here, remember? Your girlfriend? Sitting here, wondering what the hell is going on with you two?"

Roman faced her, sliding his palm underneath the blanket to rest on her knee. Logan's hand cupped her shoulder and held her tight.

"Three…two…"

"Oh for fuck's sake, Banks, we are not counting down. Say it to her. You saw her first. You met her first. You, well…just say it already."

Roman tipped her chin in his direction and said, "I love you, Ava."

A tingling sensation spread throughout her body, warming her to the core, even in the crispness of the day. She leaned forward and nuzzled into his chest. "I love you too, Roman."

Logan cleared his throat behind them, then he slowly shifted her to face him. "Ava…"

The butterflies in her stomach were doing an intense shimmy, bumping their way into her chest and throat, making her feel alive inside.

"You already know what I'm going to say, but it's true. I love you." Logan's admission didn't come lightly.

She threw her arms around him, knowing how

hard it was for him to let people in. "And I love you, Logan."

Roman's arms slipped around them both and pulled them in for a giant bear hug. One of her favourite things in the world. She nestled between them, comfortable and warmed by their body heat and the ridiculous amounts of blankets piled around them.

"No protesting the group hug?" Genuine surprise coloured Roman's tone.

Logan wasn't normally a fan.

"Not today. This moment needs it."

She hid her grin against his chest. As much as he hated to admit it, Logan was softening up. Becoming more amenable to Roman and her little touches toward him here and there. She loved it. Their triad grew closer every day, and she didn't see that changing anytime soon.

They relaxed against the back of the truck bed, enveloped in one another's arms. The sun was lower on the horizon, casting elegant shadows across the lake.

A gentle sigh escaped her lips. "I've loved you both for a while."

"We didn't want to be presumptuous, but we guessed as much," Logan said, and Roman murmured his agreement into her hair.

She slapped lightly at them both. "You did not."

"There's no other word for what we have, love. We couldn't tiptoe around it any longer."

"He's right, sweetheart."

"I know he is."

They fell into a comfortable silence, watching the sun disappear behind the endless rows of emerald pine trees. An iciness filled the air, but she didn't mind. Curled between her own personal radiators, she was warm and toasty.

Taking a deep, satisfied breath, she allowed herself to soak in the love surrounding her. Living in the moment with her two men.

No need to fill the silence. No desire to be anywhere else.

This was peace.

This was acceptance.

This was love.

Dear Reader

I can't express my gratitude to you enough for reading *Three Hearts Hideaway*. Authors are nothing without their readers, and the fact that you took the time to read my story means the world to me. If you enjoyed Ava, Roman, and Logan, I would be over the moon if you would review my book on Goodreads and Amazon, or your social media pages. Reviews are the lifeblood of the indie author community, and even a short review can go a long way. Tell your friends, your followers, your book club! And if you really want to go the extra mile, request your local bookstore or library carry *Three Hearts Hideaway*.

This book was born out of grief and hopelessness. It started as a very different project and slowly blossomed into the book you just read. Sometimes we read to escape the sadness in our lives, and sometimes we write. When I was going through the toughest time in my life, and had to take time away from my job, I turned to reading romance to buoy my spirits. That morphed into writing to occupy my mind. Two long years later, *Three Hearts Hideaway* was completed. I'm happy to say I'm in a much better place in my life now, but this story will always be one of the things that kept me going.

If you enjoyed this book, stay up to date on my next work by signing-up for my newsletter at www.lunadayauthor.com.

About the Author

Luna lives in western Canada with her husband and baby girl. She teaches full-time, and writes in the evening once her daughter goes to bed. She enjoys cooking, baking, reading romance and horror novels, and going for tea with friends.

Reach out to Luna to let her know what you thought of *Three Hearts Hideaway*, or just say hello! Find her on Instagram: @lunadaywrites

instagram.com/lunadaywrites
goodreads.com/lunaday

Acknowledgments

A huge thank you to my Instagram friends and community for encouraging me and coming along for the ride. Your messages were always appreciated (and still are). Thank you!

I have to thank my beta reader team. Emma, Sana, Noémie, Val, Shannon, Rosie, Melanie, and Mon. You were the first ones to read my story, meet my characters, and judge my writing. Your kind words gave me an incredible confidence boost and made me feel like I actually had something real here. I laughed more times than I could count. Thank you for the work you put in reading, commenting, and critiquing my book. It helped shape it into what it is today.

To all of my ARC readers—thank you! I was floored at how many people wanted to read an advance copy of my book. Narrowing it down was difficult. We all know there are a lot of books in this world to read, so the fact that you took the time to make mine a priority means so much. I hope you all loved it.

To my street team—you are all so amazing! You hyped me up, shared my posts, and spread the word far and wide! I seriously think you are all the best of the best. I am incredibly lucky to have each and every one of you. So thank you Allie, Alison, Alyssa, Amanda, Amie, Anna, Ash, all three Ashleys, Audrey-Ann, Brooke, Bex, Brit, Christine, Emma, Erica, Ericka, Kristen, JD, Jill, Kat, Kayla, Larue, Lyndsay, Nicole, Nikki, Nina, Rachel, Sam, both Stephanies, Summer, Tiffiny, Vanessa, Yesenia, and especially you, Mary.

I also want to thank my husband. You may have started off thinking this was something I was just doing for fun, but the moment you sat down beside me one night while I was writing and looked at my book and said, "Wow, this looks like a real book!" will stick with me for a long time. It was at that moment you realized I was serious. All of your encouragement and astonishment is sincerely appreciated. I love you. And to my baby girl, thank you for being such a good sleeper. You allowed me to get some writing done during nap time and in the evenings after you went to bed. Please stay a good sleeper so I can write my next book!

To my editor, Jacqui, thank you for all your dedicated work. You got this book into tip-top shape, and I am forever appreciative. The job you did was incredibly thorough and will help me in all my future books, not just this one.

To my proofreader, Caroline, thank you for

getting my book back to me so quickly! You did a wonderful job.

To my cover artist, Brittany, you brought the vision for my book to life. I know we had to go through a few different versions to get it right, but thank you for sticking with me! It's absolutely gorgeous, and I am honoured to have your artistry displayed on my cover. I fall in love with it all over again each time I see it. It's stunning. It's dreamy. It's perfect. Your art astounds me.

Also by Luna Day

Kiss and Make Love

A Contemporary Romance Collection

Coming Summer 2024

Stay up to date on my next work by signing-up for my newsletter at www.lunadayauthor.com.

Turn the page for a sneak peek at Kiss and Make Love.

A Sneak Peek from Kiss and Make Love

The Professor

"Aw, fuck me," Mr. Monroe murmured under his breath, bending over to pick up the stack of essays he'd accidentally knocked to the floor.

"Would if I could," Spencer whispered to herself, looking down at the notes on her laptop.

Out of the corner of her eye, Mr. Monroe's hands hesitated over the papers—just for a second—before continuing to clean them up.

Shit. There's no way he heard that, right? The student sitting a few seats over disguised his titter behind a cough. Double shit. She was sitting halfway back in the lecture hall. Sure, it wasn't packed with students—few people in Highborough wanted to become licensed embalmers—but today they'd had to use one of the large lecture halls due to several classrooms in the psychology wing being renovated, including the regular room for *Psychology of Death and Dying*.

She was sitting off to the side, far enough from the front to show she didn't want to be bothered by others, but not far back enough to be disrespectful to the professor. Who may or may not have heard her say she would like to fuck him. Shit again. Her and her runaway mouth. What did her mother always used to say to her? *One day that mouth is going to get you into trouble!* Well, if only she knew how true that statement had become.

Snippy. That was the word her mother used to describe her growing up. She was always told to stop being so *snippy*. Well, if people weren't so annoying, she could be less *snippy* with them. But she wouldn't need to worry about *people* much longer. One more month to go and she would be on her own, working with the dead.

Do you know what's great about dead people?

They can't talk.

They also can't hear you murmur inappropriate thoughts to yourself.

Win-win.

"We'll pick this up next week," Mr. Monroe announced from the front of the room. "Remember to finish up the chapter on end-of-life issues and decisions and we'll talk about it next class. I think it's going to make for an interesting discussion!"

Spencer packed up her laptop and notebook in her bag, grabbed her coat off the back of the chair, and made for the door before she could embarrass herself any further.

"Oh, and if you haven't handed in your essay on the funeral process yet, it's overdue. But you can still get it to me and I won't penalize you," he added, a great big smile plastered across his face.

Rolling her eyes, she pushed open the lecture hall door and slipped out. Classic Mr. Monroe. Always giving everyone extra time to get their work in. Always smiling.

Always looking so good, her brain added. She needed to stop that. Brett Monroe was not her typical type. He was too…cheery. Too happy. Like the human personification of a sunbeam. Bright and shiny and full of light.

The day to her night. No, thank you.

That was another reason she enjoyed working with the dead. Their attitude was more closely aligned with hers than most living people.

But he was attractive, she'd give him that. Even if it was in a way she didn't usually go for. Blond, wavy hair that sat tousled on his head. A crooked nose that added character to his face and made his glasses sit slightly lopsided. Thick eyebrows, ruddy cheeks, and a strong jaw strengthened his appeal. Some days she thought he resembled a dog that held his head out the car window—exhilarated and a bit mussed, but full of enthusiasm.

She would look ridiculous next to him. Him in his earth-toned sweater vests and her in her tight black jumpsuits. His wavy blonde hair, her giant black curls. His sensible loafers and her kick-ass platform sneakers.

Oil and water. Peanuts and gum. Ketchup and pancakes. Spencer and Brett.

Not to mention he was her professor. That would be completely inappropriate. Some things were best left to the imagination.

"How's Professor Smiley-Pants?" Becca wiggled her eyebrows up and down suggestively.

"Oh my god, Becca. Could you make him sound more lame?" Spencer fussed, shoving Becca in the shoulder. Rebecca was her ride-or-die, one-and-only best friend. They dated for a while in a past life, but both decided they were better off friends. Becca was apparently the only one brave enough to tolerate her on a regular basis.

"Yes, I *can* make it more lame. Professor Nice Man, Professor Tweed, Professor Sunshine, Professor—"

Spencer shot her a withering glare that stopped her little tirade. "I get it, I get it. He's not the typical person I would go for. I'm not going for him, anyway. He looks fuckable, that's all." She threw back another shot, her fourth of the night.

"Who are you trying to convince? Me or you?" Becca's question came with a pointed stare from underneath her shaggy purple fringe. "Seems like you're trying to drown something out with all those shots."

"Whoa now. Is that judgment I hear in your tone?"

"Simply an observation, that's all."

"Well, less observing, more commiserating."

"About…your sexy psychology professor?"

"No, Becca." Spencer blew out a breath and rolled her eyes so far back in her head, she was surprised they made it back around. "About Llewellyn! Every time I think he can't get any weirder, he makes me eat my words."

Becca leaned over the table between them and propped her head up on her hands. "Please tell me it's not worse than when he accidentally dropped his cell phone into the casket during that old woman's funeral service."

Spencer paused for a moment. The phone had gone off while the widower was giving the eulogy. That was pretty terrible.

"Okay, it's probably not worse than that, but it's definitely more disgusting."

A tiny squeal erupted from Becca's lips. She loved

hearing about Llewellyn's ridiculous antics whenever they got together. "Lay it on me!"

"Okay, so you know how we're not allowed food in the funeral home, and we have to eat in the building off the back?"

Becca nodded, clearly excited to hear the rest.

"Well…I cleaned last night and had to refill the toilet paper in the men's room. I walked in and Llewellyn was sitting on top of the sink, with a bucket of fried chicken on his lap, really tearing into a drumstick. Then he looks at me and quietly whispers, 'Do you want a piece?'"

Becca let out a wildly loud snort and nearly fell off the barstool she was perched on, shaking with laughter.

"You're lying! Llewellyn isn't real," she said between gasps. "He can't be real. No actual person would do something like that!"

"Becca, half the time I don't think Llewellyn is real and I've been in a practicum with him for almost a year."

excerpt unedited and subject to change

…

And if you want to read the rest, you'll have to pick up a copy of Kiss and Make Love! Coming Summer 2024.

Made in the USA
Middletown, DE
28 January 2024